TIMESPELL

HIGHLAND TIME TRAVEL PARANORMAL ROMANCE

ANN GIMPEL

CONTENTS

TIMESPELL

HIGHLAND TIME-TRAVEL PARANORMAL ROMANCE

By
Ann Gimpel
Elemental Witch Series

Copyright Page

A druid's determination...A witch's stormy rite of passage...

Katerina eats, sleeps, and breathes cultural anthropology. The only stain on her success is her worry she'll go mad just like a few other women in her family. That fear rockets to the fore when she's on a lecture tour in the Scottish Highlands and hallucinations grab her, visions rife with horrors straight out of medieval folklore.

Arlen, Arch Druid for all of Great Britain, hasn't called on his magic much in the past hundred years. No need for it in the midst of the twenty-first century. While attending a lecture, he detects fell forces. A closer look reveals the impossible. He'd thought the Roskelly witches long dead. Brutal, feral, violent, they were the force behind Scotland's bloodiest clan wars.

Risen from their crypts, they're intent on Katerina. What he can't figure out is why.

Finally! A challenge for his long-neglected powers. Far from being grateful, though, Katerina doesn't trust him. Why should she? A headlong dash to escape his unwanted attention lands her three hundred years in the past with no way out.

CHAPTER 1

Applause swelled around Katerina Roskelly, and she nodded pleasantly at the well-dressed crowd filling the auditorium to standing-room-only capacity. Her presentation on the early history of the clans had been well received, but it didn't surprise her. She was definitely in the right spot for tonight's lecture since Inverness had been a recognized epicenter for clan activity for hundreds of years.

Northern Scotland was cold and damp in the middle of December, and the days painfully short. She'd almost passed on the invitation to guest lecture at the University of Stirling, but the institution's first-rate reputation overshadowed her misgivings. A relatively new school, particularly by U.K. standards, the university's unique approach and creative, mixed degree programs had achieved staunch recognition.

Those in the front rows surged to their feet amid cries of, "Brilliant" and "Brava." Kat continued to smile and felt her face heat from the crowd's unexpected enthusiasm. She'd devoted her academic life to mapping the Scottish clans that had emerged from the dawn of the Christian era onward. Despite many clans claiming linkages to mythological gods, their appearance and subsequent growth actually had far more to do with political turmoil than divine dispensation. She'd cut her teeth on fieldwork in Scotland's Highlands and islands, and something about the misty lands got into her blood.

She may have waffled about Stirling's invitation, but the pull of the Highlands was tough to deny. She could almost believe in magic here. Almost. Her face warmed still more, and she thanked God no one could read her mind. She was being foolish romanticizing magic, no doubt a byproduct of fifteen hours in the air and very little sleep.

The clapping died down.

"Dr. Roskelly, if ye'd indulge me," a clipped male voice with a strong Scottish brogue rang from the back of the room.

She peered into the dimly lit recesses of the tastefully decorated auditorium, but she'd be damned if she could identify the speaker. The architect had captured an old-time flavor in the modern structure, and it felt soothing. "I haven't officially kicked off my Q&A session," she replied, "so if you have a question, please hold onto it." She unhooked the portable mike from its stand and walked down two steps to the auditorium floor.

"Thanks so much for coming, everyone. This next segment is only for faculty and graduate students in cultural anthropology. I'll take a brief break and see you in a few moments."

A collective groan surged around the room, but she ignored it and turned away. Setting the microphone on a table, she slipped out a side door. The crowd could sort themselves out. Hopefully, when she returned their numbers would have shrunk to twenty or so, rather than the two hundred packed into a room meant for half that number. A restroom was down a short hallway, and she headed toward it.

She'd agreed to a two-hour lecture, followed by an hour Q&A segment. Then she could catch a cab to her hotel. She had a couple of days to roam about before her return flight. Good thing. Maybe it was jet lag, but she didn't feel quite right. A vague headache throbbed behind one eye. No longer smooth or pliable, her muscles felt like unwieldy rocks. Kat located the ladies' room and pushed the door open. It was a single-stall affair, so she locked the door and strode to the sink intent on splashing cold water on her face.

Maybe it would perk her up a little. Cut through the foggy mess that used to be her brain.

A glance in the mirror startled her. Shit! Not only did she feel tired, she looked haggard as hell. Always too thin, her face had developed gaunt edges, and her blue-green eyes appeared decidedly haunted, with smudges beneath them. The mirror's surface first wavered and then clouded, almost as if it had developed a 3-D aspect.

Crap on a cracker. What the unholy fuck was happening?

She jumped back, heart pounding, but the glass grew murkier still, with silver-and-red tones skipping about like streamers in a brisk wind. Kat dipped her head into a hand and rubbed her eyes, trying not to disturb her eye makeup. When she forced herself to stare into the mirror, only her tired face stared back.

No clouds.

No streamers.

No colors.

Not hallucinating was an improvement, but where was her sense of desolation coming from? The feeling something huge and menacing lay in wait for her was almost overwhelming.

A shiver was followed by a shudder. Something with sharp, insistent claws dragged itself up her back, deepening her anxiety.

"Stop it. Right this minute," she hissed at her reflection. The sound of her voice had a stabilizing effect, but the pinpricks up and down her spine didn't abate.

Resolute, she flipped on the cold tap and bent to cup water in her hands. After a few brisk splashes with water chilly enough to steal her breath, she yanked a paper towel from the dispenser. A few blots soaked up most of the water. Her mascara had run—big surprise—and it made the circles beneath her eyes that much worse.

This time, she turned on the hot water, waiting through what felt like forever before it warmed enough to dab under her eyes in an attempt to repair the damage. Her heart still beat too fast; tension thrummed through her, turning her stomach into a knot and her throat into a desert. Thoughts—impossible ones about portals and gateways and other worlds that couldn't possibly exist—clamored for ascendency. They wanted out, but she forced them back to the subterranean hidey hole where she relegated everything that didn't match up with reality.

She squared her shoulders. It made the weirdness in her back recede, so she stood straighter still.

A very old fear gripped her. One she thought she'd moved past.

Her great-great grandmother had been some kind

of self-proclaimed witch. Or shaman. From family reports, her "magic" had edged toward the darker side of things with blood sacrifices and summoning spirits and suchlike. Everyone knew there was no such thing as magic or witches, so Grannie Rhea had to have been mentally ill. Probably schizophrenic, or maybe bipolar. Back in her day, no one labeled such things—at least not with any precision.

Mental illness was genetic, though, and Kat had been waiting to lose her mind forever. Turning thirty had felt like a gift since she'd passed the dangerous years, the ones where all the major mental disorders reared their head. With each subsequent year, she'd breathed a little easier. When she'd hit thirty-five last autumn, she truly believed she'd escaped a speeding bullet and was out of the proverbial woods.

A quick, pointed glance in the mirror revealed nothing but reflective glass. She must have imagined it morphing into a vortex, hungry to suck her into its whirling center.

Must have. No other explanation. Not really.

Rhea had been odd, and long-lived. Kat remembered the old woman leaning over her cradle and playing with her when she was a toddler. She'd been maybe ten when her great-great-grandmother died, but the woman's penetrating blue-green eyes—

orbs the same color as her own—and long, thick silver hair lived on in her memory—

A sharp knock on the bathroom door jarred her. She wadded the paper towels into a sodden heap and chucked them into a waste bin.

"Doctor, are you quite well?" a man's voice inquired. It might be the same fellow who'd spoken her name at the tail end of her talk. "I can dredge up one of the women if you're in need of assistance."

Kat inhaled sharply, blew it out, and turned toward the door. Opening it, she offered the best smile she could muster. "Appreciate your concern, but I'm just tired. Jet lag is a bitch."

The man was tall and broad-shouldered. She pegged him somewhere in his mid-forties. Straight, dark hair fell to his shoulders, framing an arresting face with defined bone structure and a strong, square jaw. A tan corduroy jacket was layered over a black shirt. Black jeans hugged his long legs, and he wore a pair of scuffed black boots. The only thing missing to complete the portrait of an academic was a pipe.

He was attractive in a geeky kind of way, the type of man she'd have maybe wanted to get to know if she had time for anything beyond teaching and research. She'd been waiting to catch a break in her schedule for years, but publish or perish was real, and she'd just gotten tenure.

No rest for the weary.

Her mind was wandering, badly; she shook head a couple of times to regain the razor-edged focus that had earned her the respect of her peers.

The man creased his forehead into a welter of concerned lines. "If you're knackered, we could skip the next part." He kept his dark eyes focused on her face. Even though he was clearly trying to project solicitousness, something else, something extra, gleamed in the depths of those eyes. His intense scrutiny sent another chill down her back.

He had her grandmother's eyes. Not the color, but the look, and the same way of stripping you bare until you got a good case of the creepy-crawlies and ran for cover.

I'm being ridiculous. Nothing a decent night's sleep won't set to rights.

Her shoulders had slumped again. Kat rolled them back, taking advantage of her height that allowed her to see almost eye-to-eye with him. "I'm sure I'm good for another hour without pitching facedown into my soup."

The corners of his mouth twitched, and he quirked a brow. "An American expression, I presume? Come on then, Doctor. I'll see you safe to your hotel once we're done here."

Alarm bells tolled, and she drew back. "It won't be

necessary, Dr.—" she quested about for his name. They'd been introduced, but she'd be damned if she could locate the synapses in her addled brain where the information was stored.

"MacGregor," he inserted with a slight incline of his head. "Arlen MacGregor at your service. And I wouldn't dream of having you summon a shuttle."

This dim hallway was scarcely the place to get into an argument. She'd deal with transport once this next part of her agreed-upon obligation was done. With a curt smile and a nod, she pushed around him and marched back toward the auditorium.

Someone had turned up the lights, and a couple dozen people sat ranged in the first two rows.

"Sorry I made you wait on me." Kat dragged a chair so it faced the group and settled into it. She spread her hands and said, "I'm all yours. No worries if we don't get to everything. You can reach me at"—she rattled off both email and phone contact information—"and I'm always delighted to entertain questions. I'm open to joint research projects as well."

A youngish woman leaned forward. Her blonde hair was gathered into a queue low on her neck. "Are you feeling quite all right, Dr. Roskelly?"

"Aye," the woman next to blondie chimed in. "You're looking a wee bit pale."

Kat batted irritation aside. Why the hell was

everyone so bloody interested in her health, never mind assuming the worst. "I'm fine." She kept her tone brisk and businesslike. "Just a bit discombobulated from the time change. I've only been here a few hours, probably should have planned to come a day early."

She made come-along motions with both hands. "Questions? Surely you must have some, or you'd not have scheduled me for this Q&A."

"Tell us about the principal differences between the clans claiming Irish roots and those claiming Scottish," a man at the end of the second row asked.

Words flowed from Kat. This was familiar territory, and the hot, tight knot in her chest started to uncoil. The feeling of dread didn't vanish, but it retreated to a spot where she could function. Another hour, and she'd be home free. A nice bath and perhaps some chamomile tea, and she'd sleep whatever this was away in her cozy turn-of-the-century hotel.

Tomorrow will be a brand-new day.

Give it up, Scarlett, she answered herself and smothered a grin. If she didn't watch it, she'd giggle and make a fool of herself in front of all these intense academic types.

NINETY MINUTES LATER, she shooed everyone out of

the amphitheater. They'd asked a lot of thorny questions that fed right into her research, so apparently they'd taken the time to educate themselves about her work. It pleased her. A quick glance at her phone showed it was closing on eleven at night, which meant it was nine in the morning back home in California.

No wonder she felt like warmed-over dogmeat. She stood and stuffed lecture materials into her briefcase. The same sense of disconnection that had assailed her in the bathroom was back in force, and a wave of dizziness swamped her. The room swam in and out of focus; she bit down hard on her lower lip. A few more minutes and she'd be in the back of a cab.

Walk, she commanded herself. For emphasis, she said it again.

Walk.

Determination could have been her middle name. Telling herself she wasn't dizzy, no, not at all, she snatched up her briefcase and shoulder bag, put one foot in front of the other, and crossed the auditorium to the main door. The presumptuous man was nowhere in sight. As she thought about it, he hadn't been there for the second part of her presentation, either.

Good. Last thing she needed was the unctuous Scot hassling her.

Be fair. Maybe he was just being courteous. No need to put such a negative spin on things.

Kat was hanging on by her fingernails. She didn't answer herself because she couldn't focus on anything but essential tasks. Pushing through the outside door, she winced as the chill damp of a Scottish December battered her. Rain mixed with snow pelted down. Damn it. She should have called a cab before leaving the building. Turning, she made a grab for the door, but it had locked behind her.

Fishing her phone out, she told Siri to find a local cab company.

A sleek, silver something-or-other pulled to the curb. The driver door opened, and Arlen stepped out. His hair was plastered against his head as if he'd been standing out in the weather, which made no sense at all. "Come on, Doc. I'll see you to the King's Arms."

She waved her phone his way. "No need," she said brightly. "I'm just hunting down a taxi." Cold water ran down her face and neck. She should have worn a more substantial coat, but too late to fix it now.

The pleasant expression on his face shifted to concern; he hurried to where she stood and hooked a hand beneath her arm. "Don't be ridiculous. I'm here. The cab isn't. You'll be soaked to the skin by the time one shows up. We're quite a way off the normal transit routes, and the busses quit running an hour ago."

"I'll be fine," she insisted through teeth beginning to chatter.

He leaned close, latching onto her gaze. "I will not hurt you, lassie. There are fell things afoot this night, but I'm not one of them."

It took a moment before she realized he'd spoken in Gaelic, a language she both read and spoke. His brogue had thickened, deepened, perhaps as a result of shifting to what must be his mother tongue. "W-what do you mean fell things?" Her Gaelic wasn't as smooth as his, but surely he'd understand her.

He shook his head. "'Tisn't a conversation to hold in this spot." He tugged on her arm.

This time, she gave in and let him guide her to his car and tuck her into the passenger side. He slid behind the wheel and nosed the car into the dark, empty street. "We'll be at your hotel in short order."

Adrenaline shot through her. He'd named her hotel before, but she hadn't considered what it might mean. "How do you know where I'm staying?" she gritted out through teeth that wanted to knock against one another.

"I'm part of the faculty at Stirling. All of us were privy to your travel plans. Lass"—he angled a pointed glance across the console at her—"do what you must to settle yourself." He looked as if he wanted to say more, but clacked his jaw shut instead.

Kat adjusted the flow of heat. Questions bounced around in her mind, but anything that came out of her mouth would make her sound deranged. Fell things and wickedness were the purview of folklore. No one with any kind of smarts believed in that shit. Was the MacGregor chap not quite right in his head?

"Part of the faculty?" she mirrored his words, hoping for additional information.

"Aye, I'm assistant dean of the anthropology department, and I've followed your work for years." He hesitated before continuing. "Your persistence and attention to details others ignore have always impressed the hell out of me."

"Thank you." Pleasure at the unexpected compliment helped allay the worst of her fears but didn't explain why he'd place any credence in urban myths depicting evil as something deeper than a philosophical construct.

"My pleasure."

Before she knew it, he'd pulled under the portico of her hotel. The rain-snow mix had worsened, so the overhang was welcome. The doorman leapt forward and opened her door. Kat rearranged the briefcase and shoulder bag she'd held on her lap and got out of the car.

Arlen exited the other side. "See she gets to her room," he told the doorman. "She's a wee bit under the weather."

The doorman nodded. "Of course, Dr. MacGregor. We'll take the best care possible of Dr. Roskelly."

Arlen reached into an inner pocket and slipped something into the doorman's coat. The gesture horrified her, but this wasn't the place to make a stink about him paying off the hotel—a hotel that was making five hundred bucks a night from her as it was— for anything extra.

She settled for, "You shouldn't have done that."

"Oh but I wanted to. Get a decent night's sleep. I'll be by around noon, and we'll go on a city tour."

Her eyes widened, and she struggled with what to say. Maybe he was only being kind, but this relationship was over and done with. She'd had enough of his innuendos about fell creatures to last a lifetime. "Thanks, but I'll be fine on my own. You've done far too much for me as it is."

He touched his wet hair in the same gesture he might have used had he been wearing a top hat. "As the lassie chooses."

Before she could say anything else, he'd disappeared back inside the car.

"This way, miss." The doorman propelled her inside. "We'll get you all settled with a nice duvet and a hot cuppa."

She rode up the elevator with him but shooed him aside when he wanted to accompany her down the hallway to her room. Ever polite and bred to serve, he acquiesced, told her if she needed anything at all to ring the front desk, and vanished down a staircase.

After a fumble with her keycard, the door finally opened. Her bed was turned down with chocolates on the pillow. A steaming kettle sat on the sideboard. When she walked into the bathroom, an equally steaming bath beckoned.

Questions blasted her, but she shut her mind off. It didn't matter if the wee folk left their hills and barrows to turn her room into an inviting bower. It didn't matter no one could have known when she'd be here to time the tea and the bath to coincide with her arrival.

Nothing mattered beyond sleep. Surely, she'd have a clearer head come morning.

She dropped her clothes on the bathroom's tile floor and sank into the steaming water, but it took a long time before the chill leached from her bones.

$\mathcal{A}$rlen was in the process of herding people out of the auditorium, making sure all the undergrads had signed in to receive credit for attending, when the fine hairs on the back of his neck prickled a warning. He scanned the room, seeking clues to his unease, but nothing untoward jumped out at him. The lecture hall, like all newer buildings, was antithetical to anything from the paranormal realm. Magic—both good and bad varieties—was firmly rooted in the natural world. Tethered to rock, earth, water, and wood. Heavy on plastics and alloys, modern building materials didn't offer much to latch onto.

He hustled the last gaggle of women toward the exit. "Mindy, Becca, Cherise. Shake a leg, gals."

Mindy handed the clipboard back. "Were you always such a killjoy?" Her white-blonde hair was cut butch-short, but she had the face and stature to go with such a stark look. Already tall, she matched his height in high-heeled leather boots.

"Aye," Cherise chimed in, shaking dark hair over her shoulders. "Why can't we stay and listen to Dr. Roskelly? We might be graduate students someday."

"We'll be quiet as mice," Becca chirped.

"Quiet as the dead," Mindy corrected her friend. "Mice toss up quite a racket."

Arlen's unease took a quantum leap forward at the word dead. He leveled a stern glance at the women. "Out. Now."

Mumbling uncharitable descriptions of him, they trudged toward the door. Once he was certain he had them on the run, he dodged past small groups of faculty and grad students who were discussing the lecture they'd just heard. He didn't blame them. Roskelly had a fresh approach to the clans, but her methods and conclusions rang true. Plus, she was that rare combination of inspired researcher and gifted speaker. Many academics were dry as dust, putting a room to sleep as soon as they opened their mouths.

As he thought about her, he recalled she'd looked a little peaked when she'd exited the lecture room, but he'd chalked it up to jet lag. Surely the psychic unrest still nagging him couldn't have anything to do with her. To be on the safe side, he loped out of the auditorium and down the dimly lit hall, noting several bulbs had gone dark. It might have been an odd coincidence, but the ugly, nasty crawling sensation moved from his neck down his back.

He skidded to a halt outside the ladies' room. Light shone around the door, so she had to be inside. He knocked, following it with, "Doctor, are you quite well? I can dredge up one of the women if you're in need of assistance."

Worry scoured him. Now that he was closer to her, the persistent wrongness that had zapped him in the lecture hall congealed, feeling perverse and like it didn't belong here. The unnerving sensation didn't seem to be coming from her, so perhaps something about her had called to the unseen world, wakening its residents. Spirits bent on mischief or, goddess forbid, nascent evil. As a Druid, he understood all about pesky spirits, about darkness too. Wicked things walking the earth just as they had for thousands of years.

Mankind could hide behind a scientific veil, pretend there was no such thing as demons, but he knew better. Even the Fae or the Sidhe or the little folk were no friend to humans. Not that he'd seen any of them for the last hundred years, but it didn't mean they'd gone away.

The bathroom door jerked open. Katerina stood framed in light streaming around her. He shouldn't stare, but she was a striking woman. Even weary, with the color leached from her porcelain complexion, her beauty smote him. Hair the shade of sunsets had been braided and coiled behind her head. Her eyes were an unusual mix of blue and green, tending toward green in the dimness of the hallway. She was tall but slender, almost to the point of emaciation. Her dark-gray suit jacket had been layered over an emerald-green silk blouse. The skirt hit her mid-calf, displaying shapely lower legs and polished black lowcut boots. No-nonsense shoes, but then he'd never had any use for women who wore high heels.

She offered a ghost of a smile, and his heart went out to her. "Appreciate your concern, but I'm just tired. Jet lag is a bitch."

The need to shield her suffused him. He didn't understand it, but nor did he question his instincts. They'd served him well, and he'd learned not to underestimate them. "If you're knackered, we could skip the next part." He watched her closely, hoping for clues. Was he wrong? Had she summoned the spirits hovering about her? In truth, he knew less than nothing about this woman, beyond her research with the clans.

The air was so thick with power, it was nearly visible. Could she see it too?

Katarina stood straighter, returning his direct stare.

"I'm sure I'm good for another hour without pitching facedown into my soup."

He smothered a chuckle and furled one brow." An American expression, I presume? Come on then, Doctor. I'll see you safe to your hotel once we're done here."

Her nostrils flared, and she fell back a step. "It won't be necessary, Dr.—?"

"MacGregor," he supplied smoothly. He might be taken with her, but she didn't even know his name. He should keep that niggling detail front and center. "Arlen MacGregor at your service. And I wouldn't dream of having you summon a shuttle."

Rather than answer, she offered a curt nod and pushed around him, clearly on her way back to the lecture hall. He flipped off the lights in the bathroom and trudged after her. At first, he planned to follow her into the auditorium, but then he rethought things. He could make far better use of this next span of time outside. Maybe he could ascertain who'd targeted her, and if she'd summoned them or they'd just shown up.

The latter case was far worse than the former.

"Sorry I made you wait on me." Katarina's voice filtered in from the lecture hall.

He shut the door leading to the hall and headed for one of many side exits. The sharp bite of power swirled around him, but it wasn't as pervasive as it had been when he'd been talking with the woman. It took a bit to wrestle one of the heavy, metal fire doors open. The weather had grown more aggressive, but this was the time of year for hideous storms. They rolled in off the North Sea and down Moray Firth. Many sailors had overestimated their mettle against such seas, and the ocean bottom was littered with wrecks.

Snow hit him in the face; rain soaked his hair. His woolen jacket would suck up water like a sponge, but at least wool held warmth and he wouldn't be cold. Calling the darkness to shield him from view, he moved to a vantage point where he could peer into the auditorium through one of its many windows.

Katerina was on her feet, gesturing as she talked. The woman had stage presence, but it didn't feel forced. She was a natural-born storyteller. Hundreds of years before, she'd have roved the countryside with a troupe of traveling bards.

Nay, that far back, she'd have been a witch, stirring up fury and telling tales the whole time.

The revelation rocked him, but also gave him pause. It had been a spontaneous sending from his subconscious, which lent it credence. He searched for holes in his take on her but couldn't find any. What the hell was Katarina Roskelly? Her surname was straight out of Cornwall, so her genetics were firmly entrenched in the British Isles, at least from her father's side of the family. With her dark-red hair, he'd bet her mother's people hailed from Ireland.

Britain was steeped in magic, so perhaps she was more than the competent academic she appeared. Although, she'd looked decidedly rattled when they talked in the hall outside the loo. It argued against her being a willing participant in the spirits falling all over one another to latch onto her.

Since he was by himself, he summoned power. Magic danced to his call, and he engaged his third eye. Ley lines, repository for Earth's energy, snapped into view. He leaned closer to the window, tossing obfuscation spells about. It would never do for one of those within to see him lurking like a perverted peeping Tom.

A single ley line bisected the lecture hall. She clung to it like glue, moving along its length as she talked. Did she know it was there? She'd almost have to sense it to cleave to its presence. The energy provided a shield. Sure enough, shadows danced around her, avoiding the glowing line.

He honed his power into fine shards and drove them through the building's faux brick wall. Like iridescent homing pigeons, they followed his bidding, diving into the center of each group of interlopers, beings that needed to return to the netherworlds that had spawned them.

His magic brought them partially into view. Winged denizens with blazing red eyes. Gnarled gnomes. Snake-like creatures with taloned arms jutting from their chests. Scaled demons with horns and forked tails. Arlen's eyes widened at the sight of demons.

It was well past All Hallows' Eve. The veils between the worlds should have thickened enough to hold such creatures on their side of the curtain. He pushed harder, intent on forcing the shadows to retreat. Sweat slicked his hands and forehead despite the freezing temperature.

He uttered power words in Gaelic so old it had long since fallen out of usage—or understanding. Except within his order. The shadows didn't budge. After a brief skirmish, his shards vanished, absorbed by the things he'd sent them to destroy.

Arlen fell back a step, mouth hanging open, panting. How the bloody fuck could that have happened? Nothing evil could stand before him, yet whatever ringed Katarina had rebuffed him handily. He marshaled his power, intent on another go at things. Strength crackled between his outstretched fingertips. His magical well was deep, and he wasn't beaten. Not by a long shot.

Before he could loose a second volley, the sound of applause reached him.

People rose and streamed from the lecture hall until Katerina was the only one left. He wanted to run for the entrance, rail at everyone who'd left her all alone. Didn't they realize how much danger she was in?

But if he left his post, he couldn't keep an eye on her. Besides, screaming about dark forces wouldn't endear him to his colleagues. They'd shake their heads and inquire if he'd had a wee dram too much whiskey. Should he cast caution to the wind and teleport inside, snatching her up? He wanted to but had a feeling such a Sir Galahad move would infuriate her. You couldn't rescue the unwilling, and he gave it 90/10 odds she'd tell him to piss up a rope.

She was stuffing notes into her briefcase and slinging her bag over one shoulder. Breath whooshed from him when she left the safety of the ley line. Shadows divebombed her from all sides until he almost couldn't see her. Desperate to help, he sent magic through the wall until it surrounded her. It wasn't much—he was too far away—but it might be enough to see her out the door.

He closed his fingers around the key fob in his jacket and sprinted for his silver Aston Martin DB5. He'd drive round by the front and take over. Surely, she'd see reason and accept assistance. The insidious wrongness clotted like spoiled cream. Something had encouraged whatever surrounded the woman, strengthened it, breathed life into it.

He sent a blast of magic to open the driver door and jumped inside. A push of the ignition and he drove to the front of the building. Katarina looked like a homeless waif, cell phone in hand, hair that had escaped her braid swirling around her. Water ran down her face from the rain-snow mixture. A smattering of his warding remained, but he caught glimpses of otherworldly creatures, misshapen and with long, sharp teeth, attacking from all sides.

She had to be unaware, or she'd be weaving magic of her own to counteract them. He tried to be subtle, not scare her, as he took her magical temperature. Either his power was failing, or she was stronger than she looked because his attempts to ferret out what she was were futile. Just as useless as his earlier efforts to dislodge the fey beings who'd latched onto her energy had been.

The chill that had assailed him earlier deepened.

Even more determined to make certain Katerina was safe, he pulled up in front of the building and shoved his door open. "Come on, Doc. I'll see you to the King's Arms."

She waved her phone his way, looking as if she were putting a brave face on things. "No need. I'm just hunting down a taxi."

The time for suggestions was over. He sprinted to her and hooked a hand beneath her arm. "Don't be ridiculous. I'm here. The cab isn't. You'll be soaked to the skin by the time one shows up. We're quite a way off the normal transit routes, and the busses quit running an hour ago."

"I'll be fine." Her teeth had started to chatter.

He wrapped her in compulsion; it was a last resort and far from a preferred one, but he was out of options. Laughter buffeted him from the darkness. It held both threat and challenge. What was out there? More importantly, why hadn't he been able to send it packing?

"I will not hurt you, lassie." He deepened the compulsion spell and switched to Gaelic. Power rode within the mother tongue, and he needed an edge. "There are fell things afoot this night, but I'm not one of them."

"W-what do you mean fell things?" She responded in kind, her Gaelic a bit on the ragged side, but he could have hugged her.

He gave the arm he was holding a tug. "'Tisn't a conversation to hold in this spot."

Maybe it was his spell, or perhaps common sense took over, but she let him guide her to his car. After closing the passenger door firmly, he slid behind the wheel and nosed the car forward. "We'll be at your hotel in short order."

"How do you know where I'm staying?" she gritted out.

Arlen kicked himself for making assumptions. Of course, that would make her nervous. She lived in California, a place crime was rampant, and people gunned down in the streets. "I'm part of the faculty at Stirling. All of us were privy to your travel plans. Lass"—he angled a glance across the console at her —"do what you must to settle yourself."

He wanted to say so much more. Ask if she understood an unquiet mind invited demonkind to enter. They lapped up chaos like mother's milk. But Katerina was shaken enough. She didn't need him nattering on about denizens of the underworld.

If she possessed magic, he was almost positive she was unaware of it.

"Part of the faculty?" She repeated his words, and he glommed onto a clear request for information.

"Aye, I'm assistant dean of the anthropology department, and I've followed your work for years." He hesitated before continuing but was determined to set her at her ease as much as he could. "Your persistence and attention to details others ignore have always impressed the hell out of me."

"Thank you."

"My pleasure."

They drove in silence until he pulled into the King's Arms' circular drive. The rain-snow mix had worsened; not a fit night for anyone to be out and about. The doorman leapt forward and opened Kat's door. After clutching her briefcase and shoulder bag under one arm, she got out.

Arlen exited the other side. "See she gets to her room," he told the doorman. "She's a wee bit under the weather."

The doorman nodded. "Of course, Dr. MacGregor. We'll take the best care possible of Dr. Roskelly."

Arlen reached into an inner pocket, and then pretended to slip something into the doorman's coat. The man was part of his order, and he'd needed an excuse to touch him. Along with the touch came instructions. He could have used telepathy, but evil hadn't departed, and he didn't want to risk any of Hell's denizens intercepting his directions.

Katerina's eyes narrowed with what looked like annoyance. "You shouldn't have done that."

"Oh but I wanted to. Get a decent night's sleep. I'll be by around noon, and we'll go on a city tour."

The narrowed eyes turned chilly. "Thanks, but I'll be fine on my own. You've done far too much for me as it is."

He touched his wet hair, angling his head her way. "As the lassie chooses."

Before she could rebuff his invitation a second time, he retreated to the Aston Martin and drove away. He shouldn't have tapped his head, but old habits died a hard death. There'd been a time when he wore top hats and doffed them to ladies.

He blew out a tight breath and relaxed what had turned into a death grip on the steering wheel. He considered calling an emergency meeting of his order. Several heads were better than one, and tonight had been one of the most disturbing displays of dark power he'd witnessed in the past century.

Who was Katerina Roskelly?

How was it possible she was strong enough to draw evil across the veil?

Even if the horde flitting about her were only comprised of mischievous sprites—and they'd been far more wicked than that—why had they targeted her?

Since he'd kicked the door to Never-Never Land wide open, more questions pummeled him. Why couldn't he sense what she was? He'd bet his last pound note she didn't acknowledge the paranormal world, let alone court its presence.

She'd sounded truly frightened when he mentioned fell creatures.

He built a ward before raising his telepathic voice.

Hopefully demonkind couldn't drill through his shielding. Power shimmered around him, turning the air translucent. Druids of old had sounded the same alarm in times of need. His people would heed the call and come as soon as they could. Many within his order were even older than him, and he traced his origins to the middle of the sixteenth century.

He drove north, heading for South Ronaldsay Island in the Orkneys. A cave and a standing circle of stones would amplify his magic, and everyone else's as well. By the time this night was done, he'd have answers. How he'd communicate them to Katerina remained to be seen. The way she'd looked at him after he offered to pick her up for lunch hadn't been promising, but he didn't care what she thought of him.

He winced at the lie. He did care—a whole lot. Something about her stirred him, but it might be as simple as old blood calling to its own. She had to possess something special, or the otherworld wouldn't have found her attractive enough to bother with.

He pounded the steering wheel with a closed fist. He'd left Thomas, the hotel doorman, with specific instructions. The most important one was to not allow Katerina to leave before he showed up to collect her tomorrow. Thomas's power should trump Katerina's desire to head out on her own, but Arlen wasn't certain of much of anything.

At least she'd have hot tea and a nice bath waiting for her in her room... He winced. Maybe it hadn't been smart to rustle up either item. He hoped she'd chalk them up to exceptional service rather than anything unusual.

Telepathic responses to his summons filled his mind. Druids were rising to his call. Relief speared him, hot and sweet. The world had turned into an unfamiliar place earlier, but he and his companions would set things right.

They had to.

The simplest solution would be to send the woman back to the States as quickly as possible. He pulled into John O' Groats and headed for the docks. The ferry would have stopped running for the night, but he'd find a likely boat and borrow it, covering his tracks with magic so no one would be the wiser. If things went as planned, the small craft would be back in its berth before dawn.

As he drove, he turned his solution about sending her back across the Atlantic *posthaste* over and over looking for cracks in it. Something about the Americas stifled power, so she might be safe back in her native California. The biggest flaw, of course, was she might not agree.

Aye, and she'll only remain safe if she never ventures onto Scottish soil again.

He drew the car to a stop in one of the parking lots adjacent to the wharf. Katerina's research was linked at the hip to Scotland. Chances of her staying put in the States were thin. She traveled to the Highlands most years to add to her research portfolio. What the hell was he going to tell her? To find another culture to delve into? It didn't work that way. She'd fallen in love with the portion of the world she'd picked. It was what made her research so inspired. That type of infatuation didn't come along twice in a lifetime.

"I'm getting a wee bit ahead of myself," he murmured to the empty car. First, he'd meet with the others and describe everything. They'd call on the magic of the stones, weaving it with their own until clarity emerged.

Arlen exited the car, locking it. The docks were deserted, and it took less than five minutes to locate a motorboat. Keys weren't important when you had magic, and he'd just fired the engine when two Druids pelted toward him. He couldn't see them, but he felt their magic.

"*Wait for us,*" boomed in his head.

He set the engine to idle. Despite the grim circumstances, he welcomed the opportunity to see his kinfolks.

CHAPTER 3

Katerina muffled a groan and sat up in bed. The covers stuck to her sweat-slicked body. She'd slept—passed out was more like it—but rest had eluded her. Dark, wicked things had chased her most of the night. Once when she'd tried to shake herself awake to evade a winged horror with five-inch fangs, all she'd done was sink into a different nightmare. The dragon-thing didn't follow her, but other bizarre hybrids popped up. Creatures straight out of gritty urban myths with scaly hides, multiple eyes, and rows of sharp teeth.

She buried her face in her hands and rubbed her tired eyes. She may have thought she'd escaped, but the mental illness she'd feared all her life had finally caught up with her. No other explanation for the past few hours. Hopefully, she'd be able to hold it together long enough to fly home and book herself into one of those cushy mental hospitals. The ones where they coddled you and shot you up with drug cocktails until the hallucinations retreated.

"Aw crap!" She made a dive for where she'd left her phone and stared at the display. Ten minutes to ten. Relief rattled through her. She had time to put herself to rights and run out the door before Arlen showed up.

Far simpler to not be here than to stumble through a series of lame explanations. The man might appear mild-mannered, but steel sat beneath his rugged good looks. When she'd waffled last night, he'd been out of his car in a trice, and she knew in her bones he wouldn't have left until she acquiesced and went with him.

She lurched from the bed, glad she was steadier on her feet than she felt. The bathroom mirror behaved like mirrors were supposed to, and her haggard reflection stared back at her as she brushed her hair, washed her face, and brushed her teeth. A quick rifle through her suitcase yielded black stretchy pants, a silver top, and a black sweater. Last night's stockings and boots were fine. She put them back on and made sure both wallet and passport were in her bag. She unfolded her rain jacket—the one she hadn't had with her last night—and slung it over one arm.

Ready as she thought she'd ever be, she snatched her phone and perched on a chair while she hunted down a local cab company. She wanted a ride to Inverlochy Castle just north of Ft. William. It was about an hour's drive, just the thing to calm her agitation.

If she was going to develop schizophrenia, she'd come to terms with whatever it meant. Surely there'd be drugs to obliterate the monsters that had pursued her all night.

After hiring transport, she debated where to wait out the quarter hour before it was due to arrive. She could remain in her room or grab a croissant and coffee from the small lounge downstairs.

Opting for the latter, she walked out of her room and selected the nearest stairwell. Her lodging was on the sixth floor, and she welcomed physical exercise. Watching where each step was—so she wouldn't sprawl on her ass—replaced needless worrying, a welcome exchange.

By the time she pushed through the door at lobby level, she was feeling almost human. She'd just ordered black coffee and a cinnamon bun when the doorman from last night rushed into the small dining room. Why the hell was he still working? Scotland was a civilized place; it must have labor laws.

He made a beeline for where she stood and offered

a smile. "Good morning to ye, Dr. Roskelly. Did ye sleep well?" His brogue was thicker than it had been last night, at least she thought it was.

"Quite well, thank you," she lied. No reason to go into any of the grisly details with this stranger. She turned aside, expecting him to leave, but he kept taking.

"I'll wager ye're quite looking forward to your tour of Inverness this afternoon with Dr. MacGregor. His family has been in this region for many hundreds of years, and—"

Kat had quite enough. She turned to face the doorman—Thomas according to his badge—and said, "Your concern is appreciated, but how I choose to spend my day is none of your affair. Nor is it Dr. MacGregor's. I've made my own plans for today."

"That'll be five pounds, six, miss," the clerk said from behind her.

Kat turned back and counted out money before collecting the paper cup with her coffee and the paper sack with her pastry. Once she had everything, she nodded at the doorman and swept past him, intent on walking out the front door. It wasn't raining, and she'd wait for her taxi outside.

For a moment, she thought he'd given up, but footsteps tracked after her. "Dr. MacGregor will be most disappointed."

Something inside her snapped. This time when she spun to face him, they were both outside. She bared her teeth in a snarl and spat, "Ask me if I give a damn. Now, go away and leave me be."

Shock bloomed on his face as if she'd slapped him. In a metaphorical sense, she had. Remorse pricked, but she refused to back down. Whatever was going on with MacGregor and this dude, who was apparently his lackey, needed to be nipped in the bud.

A black vehicle bearing taxi logos pulled into the circular drive. She bit down on her lower lip. She'd behaved abysmally. Was this going to be part of her new mental illness too? An inability to be part of polite company?

"Look. I'm sorry. Truly I am, but I have to go."

The driver was outside the cab and holding a door open for her. Kat dove through it feeling perfectly miserable as she grabbed the door's handle and pulled it closed, spilling coffee on the floor mat. The other door slammed, and the driver murmured, "Inverlochy Castle, is it?"

She nodded, realized her couldn't see her, and said, "Yes."

The cab rolled down the cobblestoned drive. Kat blinked back tears. She had to get a grip on this problem and damned fast before it got even more out of hand. She barely recognized the stranger who'd snarled at the doorman. In truth, she hoped that aspect of herself never showed up again.

To settle her nerves, she pulled an electronic tablet out of her bag and jotted notes to structure the remainder of today. In between ideas, she drank what was left of her coffee and finished the cinnamon confection. Taking notes had a stabilizing effect. It was how she did fieldwork, delineating things she would accomplish no matter what. Once those was lined up, she designated lesser goals that might or might not come to pass.

The hour passed quickly, and she tipped the driver generously for taking her such a long way beyond his normal routes.

"Would miss like me to remain?"

She thought about it. "Thanks, but no. I'll hit up one of the cab companies here in Ft. William once I'm done. I could be here an hour or the rest of the day."

The man tipped his cabbie hat and drove off down the road. The gesture reminded her of Arlen touching his head last night, as if he didn't realize he wasn't wearing a hat.

She shook her head. Why was she thinking about Arlen? She'd probably never see him again.

Yeah, particularly after Thomas tells him how perfectly horrid I was.

Kat told herself none of it mattered. Not Arlen.

Not Thomas. She'd leave a cushy tip for the doorman before checking out. Entranced as always by ruins, she gazed at what was left of Inverlochy Castle. It sat on the south banks of the River Lochy and provided a key protection point for the Scottish Highlands. Constructed between 1270 and 1280 by John Comyn, Lord of Badenoch and Lochaber and chief of Clan Cormyn, it had been built on the site of an earlier Pictish fortification.

When Robert the Bruce succeeded to the Scottish throne in 1306, the Cormyns were dispossessed, and the castle sat empty for almost two hundred years. She'd begun walking through the ruins as their history rambled through her mind.

She'd always loved this place. When she closed her eyes, she could almost see and touch and smell the many battles that had unfolded on this patch of ground. Countless places in Scotland were said to be haunted, including this one, but that designation was the purview of an earlier people who were quite superstitious.

Kat prided herself on not having a superstitious bone in her body.

Today's goal was the graveyard situated behind the ruins. She wanted to continue cataloging what she could find of tombstones. A few crypts remained. One in particular, belonging to Clan Cameron, interested her. She'd floated an abstract of a paper she wanted to write for *Cultural Anthropology* and had been given the green light.

At least it wasn't raining, and if she was any judge, it wouldn't for at least a while. The skies were gray, but the cloud cover didn't hold the blackish tinge that meant a storm was imminent. Deciding to begin with the Cameron crypt since it was her primary objective, she hustled through the graveyard and drew to a stop in front of the stone structure. Letters and carvings had once embellished its walls, but time and weather had pitted the mortared blocks. After a thorough transit, where she took photos of the crumbling walls, she drew a penlight from a pocket. Shining it on a ragged set of stone steps, she made her way down them.

A chill, sere sensation crept over her, but she told herself she was being foolish. She'd spent hours in crypts over her academic career. No haunts had ever made their presence known—because such things didn't exist. Transferring the penlight to beneath one arm, she drew out her tablet and started making notes describing the graves and urns and coffins laid out in neat rows.

As crypts went, this was one of the larger ones. The creepy, crawling sensation didn't abate, but she kept right on with her notations. If this would be her life from now on, she'd be damned if she'd allow it to get in the way of her research.

More crumbling stairs sat at the far end of the crypt, buried in shadows that had a slick, greasy feel.

"Stop it." She spoke out loud. "I'm imagining this. Air can't be oily."

Resolute, she marched to the stairs and made her way down them to a subterranean space she'd totally missed on her other trips to Inverlochy. The excitement of, maybe, a brand-new discovery, ran hot and fast. Dreams of unearthing something to add to the collective understanding of the clans was a potent motivator.

It drove her forward despite the feeling of something desperately wrong screaming a tattoo in her brain. A whole slew of Camerons—probably from an even earlier time—had found their final resting place down here. Rather than coffins, moldering skeletons lay atop marble slabs. She jotted down names and dates. Donning gloves, she picked up and examined items that lay atop some of the bones, taking pictures as she went. Mostly archaic weaponry—likely worth a small fortune—the objects also encompassed jewelry.

How on earth had these items survived? Someone should have stolen the heavy golden chains adorned with uncut gemstones, yet here they were, undisturbed.

Time passed. Maybe as much as an hour, or even two or three, before she backtracked out of the hole.

Kat fished her phone from a pocket to check the time, but the screen was blank. What the hell? She wasn't that far underground now. She looked in the corner of her tablet, but it didn't show the time, either.

Or Verizon, her carrier.

She shrugged. Maybe a cell tower had gone down. It happened. Yesterday's weather had been beastly enough to interrupt service. A quick review of what she'd written in her tablet convinced her she had enough material at least for now, and she walked through the main level of the crypt.

She must have adapted to its uneven surface because it seemed in better repair than it had been when she'd crossed it to check out the cellar. She reached the steps and trained her light on them.

Her mouth fell open. These weren't the same steps she'd half fallen down. They were in perfectly serviceable condition, the stone risers as even as stone risers ever got. The places she remembered—areas the stone had broken leaving ankle-twisting gaps—weren't there.

Her heart thudded dully in her chest, and she walked up the stairs and out into a blinding rainstorm. Being beneath ground had muffled the noise, but rain beat steadily from gunmetal skies, falling so thickly she had a hard time seeing more than a few feet.

She pulled her hood over her head and zipped her jacket to the chin. Her trousers would end up wet through, but her boots were stout and weatherproof. The storm was disorienting. She listened for the rush of the River Lochy and used it to walk toward the fancy hotel that had gone up not far from here. She'd dry out in its lobby, and maybe they could use their landline to call her a taxi.

She'd done a good day's work and avoided Arlen MacGregor too. A vague sense of guilt jabbed her, but she hadn't done anything wrong. She'd been quite clear last night that she had other plans. They barely knew one another. She owed him nothing.

He was kind to me.

Nothing more than he would have done for any stranger.

Kat sensed perhaps more than that lay beneath his chivalry but teasing it out felt quite beyond her. Besides, why bother? One more day in Inverness, and she'd catch the train to Glasgow and get on a plane back to San Francisco.

Light was leaching from the day, but Scotland was pretty far north, and days were short around the winter solstice. She splashed through puddles, glancing at gravesites as she passed them. The stones were easier to read than she remembered; no doubt a side benefit of all this rain washing centuries of dirt from them.

She peered through the gloom. Why weren't there any lights? The hotel had to be close. She skirted the ruins, coming round to what had been the front of the castle. It loomed above her in flawless repair.

No rubble.

No ruins.

The lights she'd sought burned in a few windows, but with the flickering glow of either lamp oil or wax candles. Kat willed herself to keep walking, but her feet refused to obey. She stared at the castle, nonplussed. If this was a manifestation of schizophrenia, she'd eat her notebook.

An internal struggle ensued. Part of her wanted it to not be real, which would mean she was hallucinating. A slightly larger part was fascinated at the specter of actually going back in time. And to a place she'd studied until she knew it intimately.

Either I'm nuts, or the impossible happened.

Always one to grab the golden ring as it flashed past, she was considering how to bend her current circumstances to her advantage when rhythmic pounding reached her. Not thunder. Horses. A bunch of them were heading toward her at what sounded like a full gallop. She took shelter beneath an overhanging parapet and flattened her body against the wall. Her penlight still cast a yellow glow. She thumbed it off. Fear twisted her guts into a knot, and her efforts to put the best possible spin on things frittered to nothing. What had she done? More importantly, could she undo it?

"This isn't possible." She was back to talking out loud, but softly. "I can't have fallen backward in time. That only happens in books." The whole *Outlander* series tumbled through her mind. Had Diana Gabaldon known something? How about Stephen King, H.G. Wells, Kurt Vonnegut, Michael Crichton, and everyone else who'd penned books about time travel?

The horses drew closer, near enough to hear armor clanking. Were these men coming from battle? If so, which one?

Her mouth split into a bitter grin. If she'd ended up a refugee, what better time than one she'd investigated so extensively, she was recognized as an expert?

Her hands balled into fists. Her academic brain was in ascendance because if she didn't keep a firm grip on everything, she'd curl into a ball of misery, howling hysterically. Her nails cut into her palms, but the pain steadied her. If the impossible had happened, and she'd really punched through some eldritch time warp back in the Cameron crypt, she needed a better hiding place than where she was.

Women weren't "experts" on anything in Old Scotland. They were wenches and serving maids and whores and nursemaids. Or ladies, and no one would mistake her for one of them. If someone found her skulking around the castle, they wouldn't bother questioning her. Women were expendable. They'd either send her to the dungeons or murder her on the spot—after passing her around for their pleasure—assuming she was an English spy. She spoke their language, but not without an inflection that would give her away.

Voices reached her; she listened carefully. Their speech would offer clues to where she'd landed. Part of her expected modern Gaelic because she'd stumbled into some bizarre reenactment scenario. It was a whole lot more plausible than time travel. Only problem was no reenactment could have resurrected Inverlochy Castle—or the steps leading into the Cameron crypt.

Gaelic reached her in bits and scraps. Enough for her to know she'd ended up in the early 1700s. Breath whooshed from her, and she clapped a hand over her mouth. She had to remain silent. Once the men went inside, she'd return to the crypt. People from this era believed in ghosts, so she'd be safe enough there.

Yeah, until I starve to death or die from drinking contaminated water.

Buck up. I got myself into this. I'll get back out of it.

Somehow.

Courageous words, but she didn't believe them. She couldn't walk up to the castle gate and knock. Her dress was odd. Her speech wouldn't sound right, either. Her appearance was strange enough to encourage whoever was running things to strip-search her. They'd find her phone. Her tablet. Other accoutrements from the twenty-first century.

"Fuck," she mumbled. "They'll label me a witch and burn me."

The clatter of armor told her men were dismounting. High-pitched voices joined the fray. No doubt male children from the stables. She longed to peek around the corner and lay eyes on them. See what warriors and their minions from this time period really looked like.

Fear held her back, and she fought for breath through the narrowed place her throat had become.

If they saw her, she was dead. She knew the clans, understood how they operated. A hound bayed, followed by another until a phalanx of doggie voices filled the air. She pretended she was invisible, willed it to be so, and prayed it stuck. The dogs weren't in hunt mode, so she might escape notice.

She waited, barely breathing. The men joked about a wench most of them had enjoyed. The joke was they hoped she didn't have the pox because then all of them would have hell's own time explaining themselves to their wives. One of the boys offered to stand in and provide stud service. Rather than laughter, his suggestion was followed by the sounds of a slap and a muted yelp.

It took forever, long enough for full darkness to take over, before the men vanished within, leather boot soles slapping stone steps. It was anyone's guess where the dogs, horses, and kids went. For all she knew, everyone took shelter inside the castle. Like all structures from its era, it was built to accommodate horses, but she bet the youngsters led the horses to the stables.

Kat retraced her steps, turning an ankle in the inky night because she was afraid to use her light. The injury wasn't bad, and she limped the rest of the way to the crypt and down its steps. At least it was dry within. She sank to the rock-studded dirt floor, glad to be out of the rain, which had done nothing but grow worse.

She had to do something, but what?

Out of habit, she dragged her phone out, but she still had no service.

"Big surprise," she muttered. "Alexander Graham Bell is 150 years away."

She leaned against a coffin, fighting exhaustion. Little sleep the night before was catching up with her. Light danced behind her partially closed lids, and she dragged them open. She must be imagining things. No candles down here. No flints. No other people. No live ones, anyway.

The light brightened, its edges flickering. The same wrongness that had pummeled her in the crypt's lower level was back in spades. She didn't think she had any adrenaline left.

She was wrong.

A jolt blasted her upright from where she'd been slumped against a coffin. A bitter taste coated her tongue and throat. "Who's here?" she managed, her voice thin and reedy as she scrambled upright.

"Why shame on you, great-great granddaughter. Ye should recognize me. 'Twasn't as if ye were but a wee bairn when I left the world of the living."

The bitter taste became unbearable, and her stomach lurched, painting the back of her throat with bile. "Rhea?"

"And who else?" The light surrounding whatever was talking was too bright to see through.

"Not possible," Kat snapped. "You're dead."

"Even as a child, ye were always too literal for your own good. Do I sound dead?"

Something heavy and black with sharp edges settled over Kat's shoulders. It scared the life out of her but infuriated her too. "Stop it." She infused venom into her tone. She might go down, but she'd put up a hell of a fight.

The sensation lessened but didn't go away entirely. "There's my lass. Admirable show of spirit. Ready to pick up the banner? Accept your birthright as a Roskelly witch?"

Kat took a step toward the flickering light. "Huh? What's that supposed to mean? There's no such thing as witches. Women don robes and dance around fires, but magic isn't real."

The heavy darkness hammered her, driving her to the ground. Her knees ached where they'd slammed into dirt. Something stabbed her multiple places until she felt hot liquid run down her shoulders and back.

"Take it back," the apparition screeched. The more it talked, the more Kat recalled Rhea's voice. Whatever was here certainly sounded like her.

She started to give ground so the thing smothering her would go away, but Rhea screamed. The tack-lined shroud vanished. Kat scuttled to her feet in time to see another apparition with light streaming from it facing off against her great-great grandmother.

Or the thing claiming to be her long-dead kinswoman.

The newly arrived creature was male, and it chanted in Gaelic so old Kat had a hell of a time following it beyond orders to "begone" and "return through Hell's gates." After the first few sentences, she realized he sounded a lot like Arlen MacGregor.

Light flashed and flared as the two unholy phantoms fought one another. Energy crackled, turning the air sharp with the scents of ozone and sulfur as balls of crackling light hurtled back and forth.

She squeezed her eyes tight, but when she opened them nothing had changed. If she'd fallen down Alice's rabbit hole, it couldn't have been any weirder.

The man—Arlen?—was screeching epithets in Gaelic. The air thickened, making it even harder to breathe. The light show escalated until Kat was shocked no one from the castle came to investigate. Surely flashes were visible through the crypt's arched entry. She considered making a run for it, but where would she go?

Rhea uttered a sharp, shrill shriek before her form broke apart into trailing red streamers. Only the man remained. Kat narrowed her eyes. Something had happened, but what would the trade buy her?

The brilliant illumination pulsing around the other figure ebbed to a faint glow. The man stalked toward her but stopped when a few feet separated them.

"Not sure what I expected," he growled, "but a simple thank-you would be appreciated after all the work I went to locating you."

"Arlen?" It looked like him, but how could it possibly be?

"And who the bloody fuck else would split the veils of time to go after you? Christ, but ye're a daft one, wench. How in the hell did ye get yourself into this mess? Nay, don't answer that. 'Twas your witchy ancestor pulling on blood ties to bind ye here. She told me as much when I staked a claim to you. Do ye know what year this is?"

She bristled. "Aye, that I do, *laddie*. Close enough, anyway. I heard men returning from something, like as not a hunt. Their speech was a dead giveaway." She returned his Gaelic stroke for stroke. "Ye have no right—"

"I have every right."

She raked a hand through her unbound hair, not wanting to pursue his assertion, afraid of what he might say. If it was, indeed, Arlen, and he was rescuing her from some mayhem she'd inadvertently loosed, he was offering her a boon. Boons entitled the giver to certain rights.

Those were the rules—in fairytale land.

Her head spun crazily. She had her feet wedged in two vastly different worlds, and the result was most unsettling.

The grim set to his mouth softened. "Are ye ready to leave this spot?"

Relief raced through her in a hot tide. The return of logical thought followed. "You knew how to find me."

"Aye, lassie, which means I also know how to return you to your rightful time."

"I'm ready."

"Now ye are. But all gifts come with strings."

She rolled her eyes. "Fine. I'll fuck you. Now can we leave?"

He burst into laughter. When he got hold of himself, his mouth was still twitching with mirth. "The bargain I had in mind was far dearer than a momentary tryst. We have things to hash over, important things. Ye willna run from me."

Kat's face warmed, but the crypt was dark enough, maybe he wouldn't see the evidence of her embarrassment. "This not running thing. For how long?"

"Until I tell ye we are done with one another."

An unexpected thrill travelled from her head to her toes; she shook it aside. She had no idea what he wanted from her, but it wasn't sexual. She'd offered, and he'd laughed at her. Laughed. His rejection still stung.

"Agreed." She kept her tone formal and walked toward him, right hand extended.

He shook it, his grip warm and firm. When he

released her, she felt hollow and chalked it up to living through one too many *Twilight Zone* episodes—and pathetic, fawning gratitude he was going to save her from the eighteenth century. Studying it was one thing, living here quite another.

"Ready?" He furled one dark brow.

"Never readier."

A gentler variation of the odd energy that had creeped her out earlier rose around them, turning the air incandescent. It increased exponentially, pummeling her, before it fell away. Rather than asking if he was done, she peeked at her phone. When she saw the Verizon logo and a four-bar signal, tears threatened to spill over.

But this wasn't a time to be maudlin. "Teach me how to do that," she demanded. "I managed to get there, but I need to know how you got us back."

He was still chuckling. "Frisky lass now ye're safe." His pleasant demeanor turned harsh, and he dropped his hands onto her shoulders where he squeezed hard enough to hurt. "What ye request isn't to be taken lightly."

She squirmed, but he held on tighter. "We will go to the hotel near here, the one named after the castle, and book a room. Expended power has a price. I must eat and sleep. You as well." He'd switched to English.

"If you're still of the same mindset tomorrow, we shall see what develops."

"Why wouldn't I be?"

He let go of her. "We'll discuss it, but not tonight."

"You're treating me like a child." She squared her shoulders and skewered him with her gaze.

"Because you're acting like one. Look, Dr. Roskelly, you're not an expert on everything. Tonight, you fell into a paranormal world. It wasn't of your doing, and you can still walk away. Maybe. Be very certain you want to crack that door with your own energy. Once opened, it will never close again."

She didn't know what to say, so she turned and made her way up the broken steps she remembered and out into a clear night. The rain from her jaunt through time hadn't followed her. She turned toward him after he followed her outside. "Thank you for rescuing me."

"You're welcome, lass. You'd never have found a way back by yourself. You do ken that, right?" Arlen walked by her side, a solid presence.

When she ginned up enough courage to dissect what just happened, she'd *ken* it plenty well. For now, she was doing her damnedest not to think about anything at all. Maybe his suggestion—the one about rest and food—was better than she'd thought at first glance.

"I figured the mental illness that runs in my family finally nabbed me," she murmured.

"Och, lassie. By the time you and I are finished, you'll long for such a simple explanation."

"You're not making me feel any better."

"I'm not trying to. Now, no more talk, at least not about this, until tomorrow." He latched a hand beneath her elbow and guided her out of the castle grounds.

She didn't waste effort hunting for a snappy rejoinder. She was so tapped out, it was all she could do to shamble along next to him, holding her mind as blank as she could manage.

few hours before

Arlen was driving back from John O' Groats. It was eleven in the morning, and he was returning far later than he'd anticipated because many of the Druids offered up critical information. Information he should have known, like the prompt about the Roskelly witches.

Morgan, a librarian who dealt in antiquities, had listened as he relayed what happened earlier in the evening. Before he was done, she'd interrupted, something unheard of for her, and asked in a thin, broken voice, "You say her last name is Roskelly? As in the Roskelly witches?"

Why the hell hadn't he put two and two together? Roskelly was an unusual enough name. How could he not have even considered the possibility Katerina might be related to the long, powerful line of black magic practitioners?

Within the three branches of witchdom, those who'd chosen the black magic path were by far and away the most dangerous. Arlen hadn't thought much about witches in a very long time, mostly because the least bothersome of them—humans who'd adopted Wicca as their religion—were the only visible type these days. Although some had a small spark of magic, it wasn't enough to disturb the natural order of anything.

White witches, the second group, were born into witchy families and did possess power, but made a commitment to not use it for ill. Similar to black magic, white drew its maximum power from evil, from sacrifice, pain, and death. White witches lacked the stomach to cast such spells, though, and accepted the trade-off of being contented with lesser magic. Not so with black magic witches. They gloried in creating pain and suffering. At least half a dozen families of witches were steeped in black magic, but he hadn't heard so much as a whisper from them in well over a hundred years.

Aye, and a right daft fool I was to believe they'd vanished to some other spot.

Like all convoluted puzzles, once he looked at this one through fresh eyes, it made more sense than he liked. Katerina had picked the clans for her research for the best of reasons. Her witch ancestors had been seers and mages for Scotland's clans. Beyond that, they'd become instrumental as the clans waged war against one another since the winning clan almost always possessed the most powerful witch.

After Morgan had finished ripping into him for stupidity, she'd reminded him the Roskellys had been linked to the Cameron clan most recently, but to others in earlier times. He'd bowed low, thanked her, and told her he was in her debt. He'd also silently blessed the Celtic pantheon for having the wisdom to allow women into the Druidic priesthood. The women had to be strong. They'd had a tough go of things after the Church labeled them witches in an attempt to weaken Druidic influence over an increasingly Christian population.

Though they both practiced magic, witches—even the relatively benevolent varieties—and Druids had never been good bedfellows. Druidic power was earth-linked; he liked to view his magic as pure, responsive to all living creatures. While white witches and humans immersed in Wicca respected the natural world, their more powerful cousins ran roughshod over everyone and everything.

Respect wasn't even a word in their vocabularies.

He winced and gripped the steering wheel tighter.

He'd thought the various witchy lines had vanished long ago, right along with many other manifestations of enchantment. Something about science quashed magic; it couldn't retain its grip in the face of widespread disbelief in its existence.

"*Arlen!*" Thomas shouted into his mind, a vast departure from the man's normally unflappable demeanor.

"*I know I'm late,*" he replied, trying for soothing to counteract Thomas's frenzy. "*No worries. I'll arrive in time to pick up Dr. Roskelly.*"

He swallowed hard. Knowing what he knew, he'd like to put an ocean or two between himself and Katerina Roskelly, but he didn't have that luxury. Another reason the gathering with his kin had run so long was they'd crafted a strategy. He was a key element in that plan, and the first task was to bring the witch to the cave where the rest of the Druids remained.

It was a bold undertaking and rested on the assumption his magic would be stronger than hers. If it wasn't, she'd slither through his efforts like sand through a twisted hourglass. He didn't believe she could leverage sufficient power to kill him, but it was a possibility.

As Arch Druid, he was bound by oath and blood to risk himself for his people, except he hadn't been called upon to do much except preside over ceremonies since the tail end of the 1800s. Just because it had been a long time didn't excuse him from his duties, though—

"*Arlen! Ye're not listening.*" Thomas's tone was insistent but riddled with apprehension.

Arlen shook himself. Had he been lost so deep in thought he'd missed something Thomas said?

"*Aye. Sorry. I am now. What happened?*" A deeply sinking feeling sat on his chest like an ungainly weight as he waited for Thomas to put a face on bad news.

"*I tried to hold Dr. Roskelly—*" His telepathic sending broke off, but before Arlen could question him, he continued. "*My magic, it bounced right off her. She left in a taxi after basically telling me to go to hell.*"

Arlen ground his jaws together. "*Not your fault,*" he gritted out.

"*Of course, 'tis. Ye left me a task, and I failed. 'Tis sorry I am.*"

Arlen wasn't certain how safe it was to continue their conversation in telepathy. He'd apparently read Katerina all wrong last night. Far from a victim of fell forces, she wielded major power, and she'd directed it toward escaping Thomas. But why?

"*Did she check out of the hotel?*"

"*Nay, merely flew out of here in a cab.*"

"*I'll be there in about thirty minutes. Between now and then, find out where that taxi took her.*"

"I won't let you down a second time." Thomas cut his side of the sending abruptly.

Arlen unflexed a hand from what had turned into a death grip on the wheel. Thomas took his duties seriously. It was a rare enough occurrence for Arlen to ask anything of him, and the other man must be devastated.

Where the hell had Katerina gone? Had she seen through his lightly worded offer of lunch and a tour? If so, she might have left in search of reinforcements. Other Roskelly witches who'd converge on him and clean his clock.

"Och aye, I'm being a wee bit on the dramatic side," he muttered.

Not much reason for the eighteen Druids to remain in the cave waiting for him, though. It could take him the rest of the day to track Katerina—assuming he could locate her at all. If she'd gone to ground in the midst of a pack of witches, he'd never find her.

He directed telepathy at Morgan. *"No call for you to remain."* He kept his sending terse, gruff.

"And why would that be?" Morgan asked in a tone so neutral she must be biting back further words.

"Thomas said she left, and—"

"You're going after her, aren't you?" Morgan broke in, the neutral quality in her voice replaced by

something that sounded suspiciously like terror. He could visualize her sitting in a nest of long, silver hair, her dark eyes pinched with worry.

"Of course I am, but 'tis a one-man effort. More of us would clutter the field."

"Let us know what you need from us." Sean's deeper voice was welcome.

"For now, communicate with those who weren't with us last night. Alert them..." Arlen pushed a flood of words back behind his teeth. Anyone with a smidgeon of magic could listen in on telepathic speech.

"Understood," Sean was quick to jump into the gap. *"We're all standing by."*

Sean was his second. An average height, well-dressed man with curly brown hair and merry brown eyes. He was who'd take over if aught happened to Arlen. Sean had been a banker in one iteration or another since the dawn of the Industrial Revolution. His position gave their order a quiet way to squirrel away funds. One of the sideline benefits of living long lives was most of them had amassed significant fortunes. Thanks to Sean, that money was all but invisible.

"I'll be in touch as soon as I know something." Arlen cut their connection. As he covered the last few kilometers to the King's Arms, he played the conversation back through his mind hunting for

missteps, places a wily witch could use the information to trip them up.

Worst case, they'd know he was about to launch a search for their kinswoman, Katerina. It wasn't the best news because it offered the witches plenty of time to design a counterattack, but it couldn't be helped.

He'd either locate Katerina—and have it out with her—or she'd choose to remain hidden from him, which would only boot the problem down the road. If he didn't find her here, he'd have no choice but to follow her back to California. Now that he knew what she was, it was far too dangerous to ignore her presence. She had robust standing in academic circles. It gave her far too much power to do evil by manipulating her research to whitewash witch magic.

Not that belief in the supernatural was widespread, but if people didn't think something existed, they'd relinquish any attempts to guard themselves. Black witches fed off human misery. Whoever they targeted would merely believe they'd stumbled into a run of bad luck. No one would ever guess a witch was behind losing everything they'd ever valued. Meanwhile, the witch in question was lapping up their pain and using it to strengthen herself.

He curled one hand into a fist and brought it down on the dashboard. Black magic would not see a rebirth. Not on his watch. Katerina might be part of some grand plan to place witches back in ascendance, but they'd have to go through him and his Druids.

He nosed the car into the stately old hotel's main drive. Thomas ran toward him, flung the passenger door open, and got inside. Before Arlen could question him, he said, "I found out where the taxi went. It left her at Inverlochy Castle."

Arlen brought the car to a stop in a fifteen-minute parking zone next to the curb and killed the engine. He turned to face Thomas. "Did it cost you to get that information?"

"Nay. I called the cab company, told them Dr. Roskelly's partner wanted to join her, but needed a precise location." Thomas shrugged broad shoulders, his blue eyes holding a worried aspect. Gunmetal hair brushed his collarbones. As usual, his dark blue uniform was spotless and impeccably pressed.

Arlen sketched out what he'd discovered. When he got to the part about the connection between Katerina and the Roskelly witches, Thomas slapped his forehead with an open palm. "Christ on a bleeding cross. What a dolt I am not to have seen that."

"Aye, well, I missed it too. You can thank Morgan and several others for making the connection."

Thomas drew his forehead into a mass of wrinkles. "Ye should have seen her face when she drew back her upper lip. She snarled at me. Didn't look a thing like herself."

"What exactly did she say?" Arlen leaned close, not wanting to miss anything.

"She tossed my compulsion spell off as if it didn't exist and left the building. I was reeling, I tell you, reeling from shock. I believe the next thing I said was you'd be disappointed to miss her. That was when she turned to face me and snarled, 'Ask me if I give a damn. Now go away and leave me be.'"

"Was that all?"

"Aye." He hesitated. "Wait. She did apologize right before she got into the taxi. Had a tortured look on her face as if she regretted being so nasty, but it might have been an act. Mayhap she recognized how beastly she'd been."

Arlen slumped against the plush leather seatback. Thomas's description had turned already murky waters even cloudier. If Katerina were truly an actively practicing black witch, she'd never have apologized, or looked the least bit cowed. No. She'd have cast her own spell to counteract Thomas's and been done with things. If that happened, Thomas wouldn't be sitting here talking with him. He'd be either a blithering idiot or dead.

"Are ye heading south?" Thomas asked.

"Aye. I must at least try to intercept her."

"Ye canna go alone. Give me a moment, I'll just duck inside and change. I'm not due back on shift till the morrow."

Arlen considered it. The man's additional magic might be a huge help, but he had no idea what he'd find in Inverlochy's ruins. The Camerons were buried behind the castle. A powerful witch could raise them from the dead. Something sharp and cold trailed down his spine.

"Thank you, Thomas, but this is one task I must do alone."

"But ye canna. 'Tis dangerous." Thomas shut his mouth with a *clack*.

"As head of our order, 'tis my duty. I'll be in touch with Sean and the others. We had a plan, but her actions voided it."

"She must have known," Thomas hissed. "She's a sneaky bitch, that one."

"I'm not certain of that." In truth, Arlen wasn't sure of anything, and he didn't care much for floundering about trying to figure out what was real.

Thomas didn't budge.

"You have to get out of the car," Arlen urged. "Don't worry. I'll be fine."

"Ye canna know that—" Thomas began.

"Leave now." Arlen infused power into the two words. After leveling a stricken look his way, Thomas pushed the door open and got out. Arlen reached across and caught the door handle, pulling it shut. He'd have plenty of time to consider his strategy driving to Inverlochy.

Traffic was surprisingly heavy, and it took him almost an hour and a half before he pulled into the visitors' parking area that sat near the castle ruins. The day was overcast, but it wasn't raining. Luckily, no other cars were in the parking lot, which might mean he'd have the graveyard to himself.

He got out and locked the Aston Martin before shrouding himself in magic. When he shut his eyes, he homed in on fragments of Katerina's energy. She had been here, and not all that long ago. Using his nose and magic as a guide, he followed the track she'd taken.

It led to the Cameron crypt, just as he'd expected it would. An iron bar of tension settled between his shoulder blades. If it hadn't been for aid from the Roskelly witches, the Camerons' bloody path through Scotland would have ended a century before it was finally quelled. As a cultural anthropologist—and a Druid—he knew his country's history well. Clan Mackintosh had been the Camerons' primary enemy, and it had taken over three centuries to establish an uneasy détente.

He gave himself a brisk mental shove. He was stalling, the foray into history totally unnecessary.

Determined to roust the witch from whatever skullduggery she was hatching up, he trotted down broken steps. Magic sharpened his senses, so seeing in the dark wasn't a problem. He scanned the crypt, but it was empty. Still tracking Katerina, he strode the length of the burial site to a second set of stairs.

His nostrils flared. Yes. She'd come this way. He lurched down an even worse set of steps than the first one. Longer and winding, they spit him out in a lower level. He'd visited this place a time or two and it always creeped him out enough, he'd never remained long. This room was a third the size of the one above, and Katerina wasn't here. She'd come this way, though. Her scent coated everything, rich with vanilla and rosemary.

He blew out a tense breath. By rights, she should smell of hell's bane or nightshade. Witches employed belladonna in their ceremonies, capitalizing on its hallucinogenic effects. The line between high and dead was a thin one, though.

Arlen turned in a circle. She'd been here, and she wasn't now. What the fuck did it mean? He retraced his steps, returning to the parking lot. Taking care to be methodical, he checked every possible egress point from Inverlochy's ruins, but couldn't sense her.

A quarter of an hour later, he returned to the crypt, turning the data over and over in his mind. She hadn't left the castle grounds—unless she'd teleported, and even then traces of expended magic would have caught his attention.

He made his way to the crypt's lowest level. Katerina's energy pulsed most strongly there. Perhaps it would yield clues to her disappearance. The crypt possessed an energy all its own. It washed over him, as if testing him, before power took a swipe across his shoulder blades.

The blow knocked the wind from him and almost drove him to his knees, but he pushed back. Magic already deployed, he redirected it to form a ward around himself. Whatever this was, it had the same signature as the malevolence in the auditorium last night with one significant difference.

Last night, whoever wielded evil was invested in hiding themselves and their wickedness from him. Today, the full brunt of black magic whacked him.

Dark power with Roskelly initials all over it.

Malevolent energy built around him, battering him. A whirling spot opened in the darkness and understanding swept through him.

A time portal.

Katerina had summoned a spell to bend the strands of time. No wonder her research was so spotless. The canny bitch took a wee trip now and then, right into the bowels of Old Scotland. The vortex pulled at him, its suction growing stronger.

He was holding his own. He should leave. Fuck Katerina Roskelly. He'd damn sure wait until she was back in the States, a place far harder to work magic. He could confront her there.

"Aye," he muttered in Gaelic. "The voice of reason, but I am not a reasonable man. I am here. The portal is open. It will lead me right to the witch, and we shall do battle. Whichever one of us is victorious shall return to the twenty-first century."

The sound of his words steadied him. He flirted with sending a message to Sean but didn't. What would he say? The others would want to join him, and he'd be damned if he'd put them in danger.

Nor did he want to wait for them.

An arcane summoning spell rose from the swirling place that ate light. Arlen stopped thinking and jumped through. The journey was swift, like all supernatural travel, and he tumbled out into the same spot he'd left, but far earlier in time. He could tell by how the air smelled. Dank but pure. No undercurrent of metals or plastic.

He blinked, expecting Katerina to rush him from the shadows. Instead, light blazed before him, and a woman shrieked in ancient Gaelic. This woman had silver hair that spilled to the dirt floor and blue-green, whirling eyes. Eyes that matched the whirlpool that had sucked him backward in time.

A small moan caught the edges of his hearing, and he saw Katerina standing a few feet away. The look on her face smote him. She was scared to her bones, and his interpretation of how she'd ended up here rearranged itself. The same vortex that had taken him had trapped her as well. He started toward her when a glob of magic hit him broadside. The other witch, clearly one of the earlier Roskellys, continued her tirade.

Katerina was hers. Her flesh. Her blood.

He was an interloper.

She would kill him for interfering.

"Och, and we shall see about that," he shouted back at her, matching her Gaelic with his own.

Arlen marshaled power, lobbing it back at the witch. Relief strengthened his aim—and his power. Katerina wasn't the diabolical creature he'd painted her. She'd been dragged here, which meant if he hadn't thrown caution to the winds and plunged into the vortex, she'd have been trapped in a time warp.

Trapped with no way back.

He'd bet his last pound note she'd have had no idea how to return to modern Scotland. Fueled by fury, he pounded the upstart witch who'd kidnapped Katerina. Long-forgotten Gaelic chants burst from him, magic meant specifically to annihilate witches. Giving no quarter, he piled blow after blow until her form first became insubstantial, and then blew apart.

He was sucking air like a bellows, and fury still reigned. He had questions. A whole piss pot of them, and by God, Katerina would sit still until every single one had been answered.

Not now. Not tonight. I'm too angry to be rational.

"Not sure what I expected," he growled, "but a simple thank-you would be appreciated after all the work I went to locating you."

"Arlen?" Her voice quivered, and he wanted to scoop her up and crush her against him, but it was a very bad idea.

"And who the bloody fuck else would split the veils of time to go after you? Christ, but ye're a daft one, wench. How in the hell did ye get yourself into this mess? Nay, don't answer that. 'Twas your witchy ancestor pulling on blood ties to bind ye here. She told me as much when I staked a claim to you. Do ye know what year this is?"

She bristled. "Aye, that I do, *laddie.* Close enough, anyway. I heard men returning from something, like as not a hunt. Their speech was a dead giveaway." She aped his brogue—and his Gaelic. "Ye have no right—"

"I have every right." Arlen took a deep breath, one that scoured the bottom of his lungs. The lass was scared, but like a cornered animal, she was standing her ground.

He was proud of her. Bit by bit, he felt the anger start to bleed out of him. He'd return them to their own time, but first he'd extract a promise or two. It was manipulative of him, but if he waited until they stood on the soil she'd left, she might not be as willing to agree.

Did she know what she was?

It seemed inconceivable she didn't, but she hadn't exactly embraced her kinswoman's presence. Not the way she'd been cowering from ten feet away. Her lineage opened her to enormous risk, and he couldn't let her leave his side until she understood everything.

A grim smile formed. He held the best bargaining chip of all—her safe return. Although exploitation ran counter to his forthright nature, he fully intended to maximize his slender advantage. The world did not need any more Roskelly witches.

Maybe he'd been lucky and caught this one before she made a full commitment to evil.

he Next Morning

Katerina rolled over in bed and stifled a groan. Everything hurt, but at least she'd slept well. She didn't remember much after Arlen walked them to the nearby hotel, also named Inverlochy Castle, and booked them a suite. He'd shoved her into the bedroom, told her he'd sleep on the pull-out couch, and shut the door.

Her stomach growled, but it had every right to. She hadn't eaten anything beyond the cinnamon bun she'd bought yesterday morning. Planting her feet on the floor, she raked her hands through her hair and stood. A shower would help clear her fuzzy head, plus she didn't smell all that swift.

By the time she was toweling off in a steamy room

filled with the geranium scent of custom-milled soap and shampoo, she felt almost human.

She wound her wet hair in a towel and got back into the same clothes she'd worn the day before. They were streaked with dirt and ripe from fear sweat, but all she had. She'd just finished lacing her boots when a knock on the bedroom door was followed by, "I heard the shower. Are you decent?"

Kat walked briskly to the door and opened it. "Decent as I'm likely to get," she countered.

"Excellent. Mind if I shower? I ordered breakfast for us. A full Scottish affair, so I hope you like blood sausage."

"As long as it comes with coffee, I'll eat damn near anything." She moved aside, feeling suddenly shy as she recalled her flip offer to have sex with him—and his refusal. "I'll be in the front room."

"Lass."

"Yeah?" She angled a sidelong glance his way.

"Remember your promise."

Kat rolled her eyes. "No concerns on that front. You couldn't pry me out of this room with a crowbar. I want to know what happened to me yesterday."

He offered a tight smile and walked past her. The bathroom door snicked shut, and she strode into the suite's living room, closing the bedroom door to offer him as much privacy as she could. The suite had been a blur the previous night, but this morning she looked it over. Furnished in late nineteenth century antiques, it reflected understated good taste, the décor more British than Scottish. Until she glanced at the modern rug masquerading as a genuine Oriental when it was probably made in a Chinese factory a few years back.

A fireplace graced one end of the room. When she looked more closely, she noted it burned real logs. For some reason, that pleased her. The electric or gas varieties held a far different feel than the real thing. The room's phone rang. She picked it up and was told their breakfast was right outside the door. A quick peek through the round hole at eye level revealed a smiling busboy wheeling a cart.

Kat let him in and scrambled in her bag for a tip. As soon as he left, thanking her profusely, she poured herself a cup of coffee. A teapot also sat on the generous tray the busboy had placed atop a table under the room's tall dormer windows.

The welcome smells of hot food brought a rush of saliva to her mouth, but she wanted to wait for Arlen, so she made do with coffee. It was black, bitter, and tasted as if the beans had been freshly ground.

The bedroom door opened, and Arlen emerged. Wet hair framed his face, and his chin was stubbly with dark whiskers. He'd left his jacket off, and a navy blue, stretchy shirt clung to shoulders slabbed with muscle.

Trousers rode low on his slender hips, and for a moment she had a tough time breathing. She'd thought him attractive, but he oozed a raw masculinity that made her want to run her hands through his thick mane, and a bunch of other places too.

"You didn't have to wait on me, lass. You must be fair starving."

She shrugged. "I wanted to. Come on. Sit and we can eat."

For a time after they tucked in, neither of them even attempted conversation. He'd ordered four breakfasts of fruit, yogurt, bacon, sausage, baked beans, sautéed mushrooms, eggs, tomatoes, blood sausage, and buttered scones. By the time three had disappeared, she set her fork down.

"Had enough?" He quirked a dark brow.

"More than enough." She offered him half a smile. "At home, I have fruit and coconut yogurt before I go out for a run."

"Then you won't mind if I finish the last plate?"

"Not at all." She poured herself a cup of fresh coffee and waited until he was done eating. Unlike her with her preference for coffee, he'd washed down his meal with the entire pot of fragrant, black tea.

"Much better." He pushed his chair back and eyed her. Something about his expression made her nervous, and the bargain she'd struck pricked her. So did his prediction that her worries about mental illness would become laughable—once she discovered the truth.

She sat straighter in her chair. "I'm ready for, erm, whatever you have in mind." Because she was edgy, she kept on talking and clicking things off on her fingers. "One, we've rested. Two, we've eaten. Nothing is left beyond the one-on-one time I promised."

"True enough, lass." A corner of his mouth twisted downward. "We can begin this discussion here, but we'll run up against checkout time."

Her eyes widened. "But that must be two hours from now."

"Aye."

She raked curved fingers through her still-damp hair, tossing it back over her shoulders, and waited. She'd keep her end of this bargain, by God. And then she'd go back to San Francisco and put this intimidating chapter of her life a long way behind her. So far behind, she might never visit Inverlochy Castle again. She may have had a momentary fascination with the mechanisms of time travel, but it faded fast. She was doing fine, thank you very much, at studying the past without actually being there.

"How much do you know about magic?"

His voice jarred her out of her thoughts. "What kind of question is that? It's not real."

A muscle twitched beneath one of his eyes, and the

line of his jaw tightened. "Suppose it was. What do you know about it?"

"Next to nothing," she admitted and stopped shy of adding it was a waste of time to learn about something that didn't exist.

"I take it you didn't realize your grandmother was a witch, and a rather infamous one at that."

"Pfft." She rolled her eyes. "First off, there's no such thing as witches. Secondly, great-great grandmother is more like it, and she was always...odd. It's where I got the idea mental illness runs in our family. No one would ever say much about great-great-grannie. I figured she shamed them somewhere along the line."

He narrowed his dark eyes to thoughtful slits. "How old were you when she died?"

"Around ten, why?"

"Didn't anyone in your family find it unusual she'd managed to live so long?"

Katerina winced. She'd asked that question more than once and been hushed for her efforts. "Eh, she couldn't have been as old as all that. No one lives much past 115."

Arlen steepled his fingers, resting his chin on them and regarding her with a direct stare, one she couldn't look away from. "If 'tis the same Rhea Roskelly as I battled last night, she was born in 1723. She has links to that time period, and 'twas why 'twas easy for her to draw you there."

The meal Kat had just consumed curdled in her stomach, feeling like an unwieldy brick. "Not possible," she managed in spite of a suddenly uncooperative tongue.

"Aye, lassie. Not only is it possible, 'tis true. I forced your kinswoman to give me her name, and there was only one Roskelly witch named Rhea, so it must be her."

Kat felt reality slipping away. In a frantic effort to reestablish control, she asked, "What do you mean forced?"

"Names have power. Once I wrested her name from her, it became possible to strongarm her into leaving."

"But she's dead. *Dead.* How could she be anything but a pile of bones in her grave?" Kat folded her arms across her body, holding herself so she wouldn't splinter into a million pieces.

Arlen got to his feet and pushed the window open. Chilly air blasted into the room. He stopped next to where she huddled in her chair and offered a hand. "Come sit on the divan, lass."

It was couched as a suggestion, but she recognized it as an order. Normally, she'd have told him to pound sand, but she was so far out of her league, she stumbled upright and walked to the larger of two sofas set at right angles to one another.

He nodded approvingly and sat catty-corner from her. "Good choice." He placed a hand atop one of hers. "For now, your only task is to hold an open mind and listen."

"But what if I have questions?" she sputtered, irritated at being relegated to silence.

"I'll answer every single one, but you need the whole picture first. 'Twill save time." He pressed his lips into a concerned line. "None of what I say will fit with your worldviews. You will want to chalk me off as deranged, but I assure you I'm not."

Yeah, sure, dude. It's what they all say. No one is ever guilty in their own eyes.

"All right. Let's get on with things." Kat winced. She'd sounded downright hostile, but she was teetering on the edge of terra incognita, holding herself on the familiar side by the thinnest of threads.

"Nice" and "terrified" didn't make particularly good bedfellows.

He pinned her with the same expression that had unnerved her earlier. "This first bit of time, I'll be sharing information. None of it will make much sense, but keep listening, anyway." He moved his hand from where he'd placed it and folded both of his in his lap, fingers laced.

"Two nights ago, I sensed evil stalking you in the lecture hall. It was what made you feel so...off. At the time I had no idea what it was, or if you had created it or were being victimized by it." A ghost of a smile flitted across his chiseled lips. "I'd be a liar if I didn't admit to bouncing back and forth betwixt those two poles."

"What do you mean sensed evil?" She sucked in a breath. "Sorry. You said not to ask questions right away."

"So I did, lass, but that one feeds nicely into what I was about to say next." He unclasped his hands and spread long, shapely fingers in front of him. "I'm a Druid and quite old. Older even than your kinswoman."

Kat's eyes widened; her heart beat faster, and she drew back, muttering, "Not possible."

"Aye, lassie, not only possible but true. This isn't about me, though. 'Tis about you." He lapsed into Gaelic. "After I left you at the King's Arms last night, I called a meeting of those like me. Luckily, one of my order is a librarian specializing in antiquities. She reminded me about the Roskelly witches and even drew a rough genealogy chart. According to her, Rhea was the last known Roskelly witch."

"What exactly does that mean?" Kat managed to

spit out. Her throat was painfully dry, and a lump had materialized dead center in her throat.

Arlen cocked his head to one side. "I'm not certain. There could have been other Roskellys we're not aware of, but more likely none of the female members of your family had sufficient power to join their ranks.

"Allow me a brief digression." At her nod, he went on, "The witches ye're familiar with, the ones who practice Wicca and cavort during Beltane, haven't enough power to do much with. Your assessment of them as not being 'real' is accurate. But those aren't the only witches. The Roskellys manipulate black magic. They're powerful seers and mages and sorcerers, who've even been known to raise the dead."

"How?" The single word tore out of her, and she gripped the arm of the sofa, burrowing her fingers into the soft leather.

"They feed off human misery, using its power to augment their own." He sat back, his appraising gaze never leaving her. "How are ye doing so far, lass?"

She didn't have to dig very deep to come up with an answer. "Not very well. I thought Aleister Crowley was a sick madman, a wannabe serial killer."

Arlen's lower lip twitched. "If ye add magic to the mix, he was all those things, yet he's as good a representative as any of the type of witches your kinswomen were."

"Aw shit. None of this is real. It can't be."

"The vortex ye fell through to transit time was real enough."

Her head snapped up. "What vortex? One minute —or hour—I was cataloguing Cameron bones. When I emerged, everything had changed, and I was in the 1700s."

He developed a thoughtful expression, forehead creased into a forest of wrinkles. "Rhea must have adopted a different tactic with you, so as not to alarm you. Perhaps she didn't want you to panic and fight her spell."

"You're talking in riddles."

He glanced at a watch strapped to his wrist. "Not now, but in a few hours, could ye call your people and ask them about your great-great grandmother?"

Kat shook her head. "I could, but it wouldn't do any good. Mom's the only one left. Well, her and her older sister. Both of them clam up like sphinxes whenever I ask anything about the family tree. A while back, I got interested in ancestry.com, but they were so dead set against it, I let it go."

"And now ye ken why. From what ye've said, I'm certain they know far more than they've let on, but they're not at issue here. Ye are."

"It's the second time you've said that."

"Aye, 'tis. The short explanation is ye may well be

the first female in your family line in two hundred years to hold sufficient magic to become a Roskelly witch."

An unpleasant laugh burst from her, followed by another and another until hysteria loomed.

He closed a hand over hers again, squeezing hard. "Get a grip on yourself. Now." The words held something beyond their mere utterance because the weird pressure in her chest lessened, and she gulped air.

"That's better. Keep breathing, nice and even," he instructed.

Somewhere along the line, he'd reverted to English, and she'd missed the transition. "What happened just now?"

"What else?" Something harsh rode beneath his words. "Your great-great-grannie hasn't given up."

"I don't understand." Fear lodged behind her breastbone like an ice pick. "You got rid of her yesterday."

Arlen let up on the pressure on her hand. "Nay. I merely sent her away. As you pointed out, she's already dead. Gives her certain advantages the rest of us lack."

Kat clamped her jaws firmly. "If I have this...power you claim, why hasn't it ever manifested?"

"Good question. Means you're thinking and not just reacting."

Breath whistled through her clenched teeth. "Thanks. I think, but you didn't answer my question."

"Have you ever known something will happen before it does?"

"Um sure, but so does everyone else."

"Ye've trained yourself to believe that"—the Gaelic was back—"but 'tisn't true." He continued, his tone relentless. "Have ye found things others have lost? Have ye ever followed inner voices telling you to do something, and discovered later the advice was sound?"

Kat held up a hand. "All right. Stop there. I've had my share of unusual experiences, but I read up on them, and I'm far from the only one who occasionally stumbles into paranormal land."

"'Tisn't the stumbling, but the frequency and how well ye control the results." He steepled his fingers. "Like all other traits, magic exists on a continuum. Yours is strong. Sitting here next to you, I sense it because I know what to look for and I'm trained in that regard."

She opened her mouth, but he waved her to silence. "Because ye've ignored the possibility of magic, trading it for a staunch belief in science, ye've misinterpreted many events. Couched them in scientific terms or buried them in an 'everyone does this' mentality. Did Rhea ever engage you in ceremonies?"

"W-what do you mean?" The same sensation, the one where she was on the verge of careening down a slippery slope and losing her mind was back in spades.

"Candles. Chanting. Blood rituals."

Somehow her hands, both of them, were clasped in his, and he was leaning so close their knees touched.

She shut her eyes, and his scent rose around them. Similar to what she'd smelled when he pulled her forward in time, but softer somehow. Heather, gorse, and the pungent odor of wet moorlands soothed her.

"Aye, lassie. Look back and remember."

His words were hypnotic. Images formed behind her closed lids.

An underground lair. Black candles. Rhea with her eyes on fire, drawing in the dirt with a sharp, pointed stick. Runes glowed in the dirt, white with streaks of red. "Almost there, child. Long have I waited for one such as you," Rhea had crooned about the time her mother and grannie rushed into the cave.

Her mother had snatched her up, screaming at Rhea, cursing her in Gaelic.

"Enough." Her grandmother's shout trumped everything. Somehow it even shut Rhea up. Grannie had placed a hand across Kat's forehead then, and everything went black. When she came back to herself, she was outside under cloud-shrouded skies with her mother and grandmother. Rhea was nowhere to be seen.

Kat's eyes snapped open, and the opulent suite swam into focus. "I remembered something." Her voice was thin, raw.

"Aye. I ken it well enough. Touching you allowed me to share your vision. Your kinswoman obliterated your memories when she touched your forehead, but they're never truly gone, merely locked away. I gave them a wee shove. 'Tis intriguing, though."

"What is?" Kat tried to extricate her hands from his, but he held on tight.

"Your grandmother had power to burn. She must have told Rhea to go to hell and spurned her place as the next Roskelly witch."

"Grannie didn't live for hundreds of years." Kat was grasping at straws, but she needed "normal" to reassert itself, and damned fast. Her mind felt fuzzy, as if she were drowning.

"She might not have," Arlen replied in a thoughtful tone, "not if she rejected the power flowing through her blood. Or, she could still be alive, and you're not aware of it. What I think," he went on before she could say anything else, "is Rhea attempted to recruit her and failed. Even she wouldn't live forever, so she was desperate to ensure continuation of her line. Normally, a ceremony such as the one I saw in your mind—"

The implication, coupled with his earlier statements, hit her with all the subtlety of a wrecking ball. "You were inside my mind? How?" Her voice emerged in a high, scratchy wheeze, not sounding anything like her.

"Breathe deep, lass." The soothing tone, rich as aged whiskey was back. "'Twas why I was holding your hands. Strengthens the connection. As I was saying, witches don't normally indoctrinate the next generation until they've matured. Ye were but a child in what I witnessed."

"Matured as in began to bleed?" she broke in.

He nodded. "You Americans are far too blunt at times."

She yanked her hands free and flapped them his way. "You can skip the criticism. I was just past nine when that episode happened, and I recall it clearly now. Rhea died a few months later, right after I turned ten."

"Did she try anything similar again?"

A confusing array of emotions buffeted her. Pain. Sorrow. Relief. A deep ache in her soul as both mother and grandmother made certain Rhea lived out her remaining days in an institution.

"Lass?"

"No. She never had a chance. Mom and Grannie locked her away."

"Katerina, look at me."

She didn't realize she'd been staring at her lap, and she lifted her gaze until he snared it with his own.

"Blood ties are strong. In her own way, Rhea not only loved you, she also saw you as her last chance to pass the baton to a new witch. It must have pained you when she was sent away."

Kat remembered the jagged, gaping wound Rhea's absence had torn in her soul. No amount of comforting made a dent in the pain. Something Arlen had done, or maybe just his presence, made it easier to reconstruct the past.

"She came to me in a dream right before she died," Kat murmured. "Told me she'd find me, that we weren't done with one another."

"And?" Arlen prodded.

Kat tipped her chin at a defiant angle. "I waited. And I hoped. See, despite Mom and Grannie, I loved great-great grandma, but she never came back."

"Until yesterday." Arlen's tone was implacable.

Breath whooshed from her, and she dropped her head and her gaze. "Too little, and too late," she murmured, not sure whom she was speaking to.

"Ye can thank all your lucky stars and a god or goddess to boot for that," Arlen replied. "If Rhea had her way, I'd be talking with a Roskelly witch, not a mortal woman who thinks magic is a crock." He retreated to English for his last observation.

"Touché." She forced herself to meet his penetrating eyes again. Eyes that reminded her of her great-great grandmother's. "What happens next?"

"The next part is up to you. We need to leave here. I'll drive us back to Inverness. It will give you thinking time."

"What are my choices?" She inhaled deep and held it, not sure she wanted to know.

He sent a rueful smile skittering her way. "Spoken like a true academic. You can walk away from yesterday and pretend it never happened. Once you return to the States, the odds of a repeat occurrence are thin."

"Why?"

"Something about the New World mutes magic to a certain extent. Your other choice is to embrace your power and learn to control it."

She narrowed her eyes. "Doesn't that mean I'd become a witch?"

"Aye, but not necessarily the black magic variety. You could shape your power for good rather than evil. You wouldn't be as strong, but you'd have no need of that level of magical skill, either."

She stared at him. "What aren't you telling me?"

He arched a brow. "See? That's a solid demonstration of your ability. You sensed you hadn't heard the whole story. And you haven't. If you decide to open the door to your power, I can almost guarantee another confrontation with Rhea. She will demand you pick up the threads of your birthright, and you'll have to be strong enough to refuse."

"Why would it even be a problem?"

He shrugged. "Power corrupts, lass. Absolute power—"

"Corrupts absolutely," she finished for him, and then added, "but I'd have to want what she's offering."

"Indeed." He got to his feet and extended a hand, hauling her upright. "Witchy magic could propel you to the tip top of your field."

"Meh. I'm already almost there, and I did it on my own."

"Witch power could make you rich."

She shrugged. "Money is overrated. Besides, I have enough."

He frowned. "You're being flip. This is the most serious decision you've ever faced, but at least you're tackling it as an adult and not a vulnerable nine-year-old. Give this twenty-four hours to percolate, and we'll revisit it."

She went into the bedroom and collected her bag and briefcase, her mind brimming over with questions.

Uppermost was why she'd stopped questioning his primary assertion: that magic existed in the world. Every single thing he'd said rested on that claim.

Kat returned to the suite's living area. "I'm ready."

"Good time to make a run for the car." He grinned as if they hadn't spent the last couple of hours discussing the impossible.

She peered out the still open window. "Why would you say that? It's raining."

He shrugged. "Merely misting, lass. Shall we?" He pulled the door open and motioned her through.

rlen had forestalled further conversation while they drove north. He'd left Katerina at the King's Arms with stern instructions to eat again and get some rest. She'd asked where he was going but retracted the query almost immediately. He understood, or he thought he did. Her question presumed an intimacy where they had a right to know one another's whereabouts, yet nothing had passed between them.

He blew out a breath, followed by another. Perhaps it was a byproduct of her magic, but he was drawn to her, attracted to her so strongly, his need shocked the hell out of him.

And it wasn't precisely true that nothing had passed between them. He'd relayed a tale worthy of *Grimm's Fairytales*, the original, bloody version that hadn't been sanitized for modern children. Myth and fantasy aside, the desire to shelter her and protect her was strong, but odds were he'd have to bury his longing and watch her walk away. As soon as the thought marched across his mind, he realized he fully expected her to run from her nascent power. She'd lived thirty-five years without delving into that part of her nature, which meant she was stronger than the Alice in Wonderland trapdoor in her mind.

Before he drove away, after telling her he'd pick her up at seven sharp for supper, she'd said she was going to remain a day or two longer than her original plans. Joy had speared him at the prospect of more time with her, but he chided himself as he guided the car through light midafternoon traffic.

Where she went, and what she did, were none of his affair.

He'd have to be very careful not to do anything to influence her decision about her magic. She had to come to terms with what she wanted on her own without any pressure from him. Power could be a perilous path—and a great responsibility. It wasn't something to be undertaken lightly.

He hadn't been joking when he'd told her the choice was irrevocable. She couldn't go backward if the going got rough.

"Arlen?" Sean's telepathy sent guilt ratcheting through him.

"Aye. I'm fine. Sorry. I should have contacted you before this."

"No worries. Feel like a spot of tea?"

Arlen grinned. It was Sean's way of requesting a meeting, one where he could mine for details about Katerina. He started to decline, but his initial resistance yielded to common sense. Sean had a shrewd, incisive mind. He'd be a good resource, and he wouldn't mince words if he felt Arlen had made a huge mistake disclosing magic to someone who was mostly human.

Katerina had magic aplenty, but for all intents and purposes she counted as magically naïve: ergo human.

"Well?" Sean pressed.

"Sure. Usual spot?"

"Aye. Where else? I'm already there. See you soon." Sean closed their connection.

Arlen had been heading home. He turned the Aston Martin back toward town. The car was one of his few indulgences. If he spent willy-nilly for the next hundred years, he'd be hard pressed to run through his funds. As it was, he walked a fine line between surrounding himself with nice things and not appearing so ostentatious people gossiped about him being a spendthrift.

Scotsmen were a frugal people. Flashy and flamboyant never met with approval, nor did spending. Saving was valued to the extent it was almost a national pastime. When he'd decided to remodel his two-hundred-year-old manor house, he'd spread the project out over a decade, and turned the rather austere structure into something warm and inviting.

His mind was wandering, but he needed a break. He'd trod a fine line with Katerina. He couldn't soft-pedal what she was to the point she didn't take him seriously. Nor did he want to terrify her. As it was, he'd seen her fear, felt it leak from her pores. She was a strong woman, but no one was strong in the face of something so alien it flew in the face of everything they'd ever believed in.

He'd felt her fascination at the prospect of time travel. It didn't take much of an imagination to see wheels turning in her head and her coming to the inescapable conclusion it would be easier to study the past if she were actually there.

Hope spilled through him, but he pushed it aside. He'd have to make certain she understood using magic for that type of thing was forbidden. Maybe not for black magic practitioners, but certainly for those like him who walked the good side of the magic street.

They lived in a human world. Employing magic to gain an advantage over humans was strictly prohibited.

He pulled into the small parking lot behind Sean's favorite tea shop and bakery. Delightful smells wafted over to him the moment he exited his car, and he hurried inside.

Sean raised a hand in greeting from his usual spot in the far back corner. Arlen stopped by the counter and purchased a pot of tea and two scones with butter and marmalade. The clerk assured him she'd bring everything to his table, so he trotted to the end of the room and slid into the vacant chair.

"Cheers!" Sean waggled his teacup in Arlen's direction.

"Cheers, back at you."

Sean spun an index finger in a circle. "I'm all ears, mate." He switched to an antiquated form of Gaelic, and Arlen felt the faint touch of a spell designed to keep their conversation within its bounds.

He shook his head and smiled encouragingly at a youngish blonde woman wearing an apron who was heading their way with a loaded tray. "Wait until my tea and biscuits show up."

"Of course. Wouldn't want you to go hungry." He pinned Arlen with his keen dark eyes but stopped before mentioning how magic sapped a person.

Arlen pressed a one-pound tip into the serving girl's hand and cracked the lid on the teapot. As was usual in this establishment, the tea was already perfectly steeped. He poured himself a cup, adding sugar as he felt Sean's spell settle around them again.

"I'll save you the trouble of peppering me with questions," he said and sketched out his journey to Inverlochy, both in this time and the earlier one. Borrowing from Sean's example, he switched to Old Gaelic as well.

Normally imperturbable, Sean stared at him, eyes rounding as the tale played itself out. "Och aye, how did ye determine just where in time ye landed?"

"'Tis a fair question. I knew 'twas much earlier because the very air had a different tang, but mostly I put two and two together. Rhea would be strongest in her original time period, and Katerina was out and about long enough to overhear men talking."

"I see." Sean nodded. "With her background studying the clans, she'd have been able to hear their Gaelic and pin the era quite accurately." He set his cup down and took a thoughtful bite of a French pastry. "It's encouraging she didn't run screaming from the room. Ye told her a lot."

"No more than was absolutely necessary." Arlen defended himself. Under typical circumstances, a quorum of Druids would decide how to proceed in the face of someone who didn't believe in magic but carried the ability to wield it if they chose.

Sean raised one hand, palm facing out in a

conciliatory gesture. "I wasn't criticizing you. Hell, mate, I'm impressed as hell ye got as far as ye did with a midcareer academic. Do ye have any idea what she'll decide?"

Arlen shook his head. "I'm taking her to dinner in a couple of hours. If she has more questions, I'll answer them. She was running on overload in Ft. William, and I didn't think it would be productive to keep on talking there."

"Ye have a stake in this."

It wasn't a question. Arlen considered disputing his old friend's assumption but gave it up for lost effort. Sean had known him far too long and understood him far too well.

"Aye, but I will not influence the outcome."

"Good. 'Tis a difficult path we've chosen, not one without rewards, but still it does complicate things." He frowned. "For her to get up to snuff at this point in her life will take years."

Arlen slathered butter and marmalade on a scone and took a generous bite, chewing and swallowing thoughtfully. "Years, indeed, and 'twill be harder for her than for most because she'll be fighting against simply summoning the magic she was born to and being done with it."

"Aye. The darker side of things."

Arlen nodded and ate more of his scone.

"Depending on how things go over dinner, ye might consider bringing her out to the island. I could ensure a few of us are at the stones."

Protectiveness surged, hot and primitive. Arlen dialed it back. His people weren't whom she needed to guard against.

"We'll see how it goes," he replied.

"The great-great-grandmother, Rhea. She'll try again," Sean said.

"Och and tell me something I don't know." Arlen popped the last of the scone into his mouth. He chewed and swallowed, savoring its buttery layers.

Sean stood and clapped Arlen across the back; his spell dissipated "We'll be at the stones on South Ronaldsay, and we'll remain until midnight. Let me know if ye need aught from us."

Arlen stood too and gripped Sean's hand. "I shall. I'll also make certain ye know if we're headed your way, so ye don't wait on us for naught."

"I'll let the others know." Sean switched back to English, released his hand, and strode from the coffee shop. His impeccably tailored Italian suit flowed around his retreating form.

Arlen sat, intent on finishing his tea and the remaining scone. Gratitude for Druids and their fellowship beat a path through him. If Katerina picked magic over her old life, he'd make certain she didn't go it alone. He wasn't quite sure how that would play out. There were Druid societies in the States, but would they accept a witch?

Whoa. I'm getting a wee bit ahead of the curve.

He needed to wait, give her all the space in the world. If she ended up choosing her old life, he'd do what he could to bury her memories, so they didn't torment her. Unfortunately, he'd be one of the casualties, right along with what he'd told her about witch power. No way to separate the two.

Frustration soured his stomach, and he dropped the other half of the second scone back onto its waxed paper doily. For a bright man, he'd just done a very stupid thing.

Not as dumb as all that, he told himself. He couldn't link himself to a mortal. He might yearn for her, but building a life with someone without magic wasn't possible. He'd watched many Druids fall in love with humans, and it never ended well. Naught but heartbreak lay along that course.

He'd have to soft-pedal what he was.

She'd die far too soon. Not embracing her witch heritage shackled her to a normal human lifespan...

A glance at his watch told him he barely had time to run home and change before dinner. Grateful to have something to do—other than longing for Katerina —he stood and hurried outside to his car.

Stripping her fledgling knowledge about magic held its own set of risks. Ones that had nothing to do with him. Sean had been right on target when he'd said Rhea would try again. Something had apparently altered in the paranormal realm, and the old witch was stronger than she had been. Strong enough to make a play for her blood kin. Whether she'd be able to launch another attack in the States was an unknown.

Arlen's thoughts whirled from point to point, bouncing off one another. Maybe Rhea wasn't stronger at all, but Kat's proximity here in the U.K. had spawned her strike. He stared through the windscreen, driving on autopilot. Katerina traveled to the U.K. at least annually, and Rhea hadn't bothered her before.

Why now?

He touched an electronic device, and ten-foot wrought-iron gates opened. Usually, his home was a peaceful spot, but he had too many unanswered questions to relax. He had to guess—and guess right— about a lot of things. If he didn't, Rhea's next effort might snag Katerina.

She loved the old woman. He'd seen the pain in her soul when she'd told him what happened to her great-great grandmother. Witches were an unscrupulous lot, and Rhea would leverage any quarter if it meant paving a path for the next Roskelly witch.

Something cold and slimy slithered down his spine

as he got out of his car and sprinted inside. Arlen doubled up a fist and shook it. He hated premonitions of evil lurking in the wings because they so often came true.

KAT WAS WAITING for him when he pulled into the King's Arms' circular drive. Relief rattled from his head to his feet, and he understood he'd been afraid she was going to ditch him just like she'd done the previous day. Her presence was a mixed bag, though, because it meant the bad thing he'd sensed was something other than her vanishing again.

She pulled the passenger door open before he could get out and hold it for her. "Whew. Didn't know if I'd get back in time."

Alarm bells tolled. He didn't want to come off as heavy-handed, so he tried for casual as he asked, "Where'd you go?"

"Just to buy a few things. I only packed for two days. It's easier when I travel light. That way, I don't have to deal with checking any luggage—and the airline losing it."

He guided the sports car back into moderate traffic and bit back a lecture on how it wasn't safe for her to be out and about. It might not be, but he didn't want to turn her into someone who was afraid to leave her hotel, either. "What kind of food do you like?" He glanced across at her. The strained look wasn't as pronounced, but dark smudges still rode beneath her eyes.

She shrugged. "Most anything. I'm not big on fancy dining, but I like ethnic food."

"East Indian okay?"

She chuckled, and the sound warmed him. "You've got my number, bud. I never met a curry I didn't like."

"I know just the place. How are you feeling?"

"Wiped out, but then I figure it will take more than a night's sleep and a few meals to put everything in perspective."

He waited, determined not to influence her in any way. If she began talking about magic, great. If not, he could wait. Not forever, though. She needed to know how to ward herself.

Back off. His inner voice was stern. He had an agenda—teaching her to use her power—but she had a host of most excellent reasons not to share it.

"Is anything wrong?" She turned toward him.

"No. I just have a lot on my mind is all." He hesitated before adding. "All those other times you've been in the U.K., has—"

She saved him the trouble of picking neutral words by interrupting him. "Rhea's never shown up before.

I've turned that one over and over because it makes no sense. You said magic has a harder time flourishing where I live, so that might explain why she never bothered me in California."

"Aye, but it doesn't cover the times you've been here."

She blew out a noisy breath. "Precisely. Anyway, I had an idea."

Something about her tone clued Arlen he wouldn't care much for it, so he opted for a joke. "Och aye, lassie. Women aren't supposed to clutter their heads with such things."

"Pfft. I want you to teach me how to time travel. Maybe if I go back to where Rhea is, talk with her—"

Arlen pulled the car into a handy parking spot. They were still a couple of blocks from the restaurant, but it was easy walking distance. He centered the Aston Martin between two other cars before he trusted himself to say, "'Twould be verra dangerous for ye to do that." His brogue was thick, which told him how upset he was.

He reached across the console and clasped one of her hands in his. Her fingers were cold, so she must understand how risky her suggestion was.

"Lass. Listen to me. If ye chose to embrace the power within you, 'twill take months afore ye have any facility with it, mayhap longer. During that time, ye'll be vulnerable as a newborn."

A mulish look formed on her face. Before she could tell him to go to hell, he forged ahead. "That ritual ye have memories of. Rhea never got to the part where she carved a chunk out of your arm and fed it into the cauldron I saw in your vision, along with snakeskin, eye of newt, and a few other prime ingredients. The incantation would have sealed your fate as a dark magic-wielder, a sorceress as it were."

Kat's expression altered from stubbornness to revulsion. "Great-Great-Grannie wouldn't have done that. She loves me."

Arlen got hold of himself. Which was more important? Preserving Kat's memories of her great-great-grandmother, or making certain she fully understood how serious yesterday had been?

He didn't have to think long. "Of course, she loves you, but she loves her allegiance to the Roskelly witch line more. Ye studied the Camerons. I've read some of your papers. Do ye recall their seers? Their wise women? The ones who were always skulking about on the sidelines during every important battle?"

He tightened his grip on her hand, but she didn't pull away. "There wasn't anything about wise women —or witches—in any of the accounts I read. Nor were Roskelly women buried in the crypt."

"They wouldn't have been. The Camerons used the Roskelly witches to their benefit, leveraging their power to mow through rival clans." He paused for emphasis before adding, "Drawing on the witches' power and viewing them as equals are two different matters entirely."

Katerina dragged her gaze up to meet his. "What did the witches get out of the deal?"

"They avoided the hangman's noose or being burned. Witches didn't fare well once the church grew strong."

She squeezed her eyes shut for a long moment. "Talk about a stupid question. I'm not firing on even close to all cylinders. I suppose it's also why I never read about any witches or sorcerers or magic of any kind. If the Camerons admitted to using such tricks, they'd have been censured by the Church, forced to abandon their wicked ways."

Arlen offered her credit for jumping to the right conclusion, but she'd studied old Scotland as extensively as anyone. "I want to say one more thing, and then I suggest we eat. If you return to Inverlochy's ruins, there's a good chance the same thing would happen again. Rhea would pull you through to her time. She figured out how to do it once, so the next attempt would cost her even less magical output.

"Once there, though, you'd be stuck. She'd be far more careful to guard against losing you."

Kat tilted her chin at a defiant angle. "You could come with me."

"Your faith in me is touching, but my magic is no match for hers."

"You beat her once."

Something about her tone warmed him. "I got lucky. Might not be so fortunate a second time." He didn't add Rhea would bring reinforcements. Witches had no trouble manipulating power from beyond the grave, and there were a whole lot of dead Roskelly witches.

"Teach me, then. You say I have magic. Maybe with both of us—"

She was so intense and so lovely and so determined, the reserve he habitually used as a shield crumbled. Her spirit sang to him, and he yearned to possess her. He shut off everything but the moment, leaned across the console, and crushed his mouth over hers. He had no idea how she'd react, and he half expected her to wrench her body away.

Instead, she kissed him back, tasting of summers and promise and hope, things he'd left behind long since. Her lips were full and firm as they traded bites with kisses, tongues sparring with one another. Bent at an uncomfortable angle, his cock thickened and pressed against his trousers.

What he was doing felt wrong, but also right in a way little else had in his long life. He'd never married because duty to the Druids overshadowed everything. Kissing Kat wasn't about duty or Druidism or any of the other things that filled his days. It was indulgent and sweet and hot and amazing. Even with the console between them, she molded her upper body against him, and the press of her full breasts tantalized him. What would she look like naked? How would she feel as he sank into the dark, slick mysteries between her legs?

Once fantasies of fucking her engulfed him, he tugged his mouth from hers. If he didn't stop now, he might not be able to. His heart hammered against his chest, and he was breathing hard. The sexual part of his nature rarely got any airtime, and his cock and balls ached and throbbed, reminding him they resented the hell out of being discounted.

Katerina pulled away, eyes glittering with lust and longing. "We'd best get that dinner well in hand." She sounded breathless, and evidence of her arousal thrilled him.

She wanted him too.

He laughed softly. "Aye, or we'll end up in the back

seat for a wee tumble, and it's far too small to offer much in the way of comforts."

"Somehow"—she ran her tongue over her lower lip—"I don't think we'd notice."

He released her hand and got out of the car, meaning to come around to her side, but she was already standing on the curb, bag slung over one shoulder, waiting for him. He slipped a hand under her elbow and steered her toward the restaurant. It had many secluded tables tucked into dark corners, but maybe it would be better not to tempt fate with too much privacy.

She was a damned attractive woman, and she had a whole lot on her plate. Adding an affair to the equation would be foolhardy. As if she read his thoughts, she leaned into him. Her scent, vanilla laced with rosemary, was heady, and he breathed it in.

He started to tell her the kiss had been a mistake, that he'd been presumptuous, but he couldn't quite get the words out. Katerina might not be aware of her magic on a conscious level, but she could spin a love charm with the best of her departed kin. Now that he was looking for it, he felt its subtle edges nudging him.

The chill that had assailed him earlier trickled down his spine in warning, and his erection subsided fast. Something was very wrong here, and he had to figure out what it was before too much more time passed. He'd come within an angstrom of unzipping his pants and having her straddle his lap.

No more kisses. Hell, no more hand-holding. Not until I sort this out.

They reached the restaurant, and he held the door open for her. Once within, he requested a brightly illuminated table. Confusion, disappointment, and hurt feelings swirled through her mind. He did his damnedest to redirect her with neutral questions about the Inverness clans. Her automatic answers held a chilly edge, but at least the love charm dissipated.

He'd have to be far more cautious until he knew more. She might not wield power consciously, but her magic burned so bright it formed a conduit. One that could come back to bite them both in the ass.

CHAPTER 7

Katerina trudged up six flights to her room. Arlen had been unfailingly pleasant and proper through dinner, but the brief chink in his persona that had surfaced when he kissed her had sealed itself so thoroughly she questioned whether the kiss had even happened. The restaurant had plenty of out-of-the-way corners, but he'd asked the maître d' to seat them in a well-lighted spot.

Clearly, he regretted kissing her. Did he have a wife stashed in a medieval manor house? Or maybe a girlfriend or two? He didn't seem the philandering type, but he was a man, and they had a habit of thinking with their dicks.

She flashed her key card over the scanner, and the door to her room popped open. As she walked inside, she corrected herself. If he'd been out to exercise his appendage, they'd have ended up in bed. He might think with his cock, but he didn't give it the upper hand.

She winced. This made twice she'd offered herself up.

"And twice he turned me down." She kicked the door shut behind her, feeling like the slut of the year.

After wading through his thoughts about the local clans, she'd asked a lot of questions about magic over their meal. He'd answered them all, while cautioning her to take a few more hours before she set what would be an irrevocable course.

Irrevocable.

Arlen had used that word so many times, she'd wanted to scream at him to pick something different. Binding, for example. Or irreversible or unalterable or unchangeable.

She slumped into an easy chair pushed into a corner. She should kick off her boots, but she didn't feel like bending to unlace them. The problem she'd pointed out earlier, the one about why Rhea had shown up now and not on any of her other trips to the U.K., festered.

If she could figure it out, she might have an edge. Despite Arlen's graphic description of the ceremony her mother and grandma had interrupted, she couldn't make herself believe Rhea would be so cold-blooded as to lock her into a future without any choices.

I suppose she thought it was best for me.

Even so, Kat answered herself, *I was a child. No nine-year-old has the maturity to agree to a lifetime commitment to sorcery. Or anything else.*

A chill, uncomfortable sensation slithered down her spine, almost as if something she couldn't see was loose in the room. She scanned the well-lit space, but nothing amiss jumped out at her.

She fished in her bag for her tablet and brought up the Internet, typing in Druid to freshen her knowledge base. Maybe Arlen had been wrong about her great-great grandma. No reason for Druids to know much about witches…

The unpleasant feeling left, replaced by something warmer. The creeped-out feeling she wasn't alone persisted, but she shoved it aside to concentrate on the articles populating across her screen.

Time passed. She made notations as she read, grateful she had access to academic archives. After an hour, she'd come to the conclusion there were two distinct interpretations of Druidism, one linked to pagan practices and mythology, and the other whitewashed behind a veneer of modern rationalizations. If the former was to be believed, Arlen could certainly know a whole hell of a lot about witchcraft, since a Druid's primary task was to provide a shield against evil and keep it from seeping into the world.

Breath whistled from between her clenched teeth. She sagged against her chair and relaxed her jaw. The other realization she'd come to was that while she viewed nine-year-olds as children, it hadn't been the prevailing view three hundred years ago. If Rhea was actually born in 1723—a fact Kat was still having trouble wrapping her mind around—she hailed from an era when children were treated as smaller versions of adults. No one lived very long, and youngsters began working as soon as they could fold their pudgy little fingers around rakes, hoes, and other tools.

"Why am I making excuses for her?" The sound of her voice startled Kat, but she kept talking out loud to the empty room.

"Because I can't let go of her caring about me. It's really hard to envision her as a cold-blooded Svengali, who only wanted to use me to further her own agenda."

A bitter laugh spewed from her. She persisted in viewing everything in modern terms when she'd be far better off adjusting her perceptions. This wasn't about how things were now, but about how they'd been historically.

Like her revelation about children working almost from the time they could walk.

She felt antsy. Sitting any longer wasn't in the cards, so she laid her tablet on a nearby table and got to her feet. She should try to sleep, but she was too wound up. Maybe a walk would be just the thing to settle her. It wasn't even ten o'clock yet. Probably not too late for a stroll.

She shrugged back into her raincoat, gathered her bag and her electronics, and let herself out into the quiet, carpeted hall. Not wanting to run into anyone, she took a back staircase and a little-used rear entrance. Kat was halfway down the block before it dawned on her she'd been afraid she'd run into Thomas. He'd worked the night shift before.

She slowed. What would have been wrong with seeing him? She owed him an apology for how badly she'd treated him. Feeling torn, she stopped, unsure whether to go back and find the doorman or press on.

What the hell was wrong with her? She usually didn't have any trouble deciding what to do. Nor did she have issues sleeping. Making a firm commitment to seek out the doorman later, she pushed on, walking fast.

She felt odd, unsettled. Like herself, yet not. The eerie bifurcation that had begun in the lecture hall was growing steadily worse. The only time she truly regained her sense of who she was had been when she was with Arlen.

Why? Did something about his Druid blood keep her demons at bay?

The dark, cloud-shrouded night pulled closer to her, and she shivered. "For Christ's sake, get a grip," she muttered. "Nothing's changed about the night. It's the same as it was when I left the hotel."

A man dressed in evening clothes and a topcoat strode past her. "Are you quite all right, miss?"

"Fine." She snapped off the word. Damn it. He must have heard her. She needed to keep her mouth shut.

After angling a concerned glance her way, he nodded and kept walking.

She really should go back. The stroll was supposed to settle her nerves, but it was having the opposite effect. She was about to turn around when the bulk of Inverness Castle rose before her. On a cliff overlooking the River Ness, the red sandstone building was built around 1836 on the site of an eleventh century fort. Several castles had resided on this spot between the first one and now.

Kat knew their history well, reciting it to herself.

The calm that had eluded her returned in a welcome cascade of normalcy. Maybe a ramble around Inverness Castle was just the ticket. Ruins were where she lived, and although the current structure was far from a crumbling shell, she felt its history in her bones. The same singlemindedness that had served her well as an anthropologist arrowed through her, and she worked her way around the building.

It had been closed to the public for years, but she'd gotten inside on a previous trip by flashing her academic credentials. The subbasement area had been fascinating, complete with what was left of dungeons and medieval torture rooms. A paper she'd compiled from her visit had received critical acclaim from her peers, but she'd loved doing the research. Digging into old things, determining how cultures operated, fed her soul.

Smiling to herself, she reached out and dragged her fingertips along the rough outer wall. The darkness shattered around her, and she pitched forward. Screams crowded the back of her throat. When they emerged, they weren't much more than high, piercing yips.

The sensation of falling brought on vertigo, but how could she be falling when she still stood, feet planted firmly beneath her. The fingers touching the wall were so cold they ached. In a dull, distant spot she recalled everything going to hell as soon as she touched the stone. She tried to yank her hand back, but it refused to budge.

The screams did come then. One after the other as blackness closed around her. The falling sensation escalated, and she landed with a spine-jarring thud. Kat forced her eyes open, not knowing when she'd closed them. It was still night. Still cold. Not raining.

Maybe she'd gotten lucky.

The moment she took in Inverness Castle—an obviously earlier version of the stately structure—she knew she hadn't. A quick sniff yielding raw sewage, poorly cured leather, and horses confirmed her fears. She may have been blindsided before but courtesy of her last involuntary jaunt through time, she knew exactly what had happened. Hopefully, she'd missed the siege on the castle in 1715, and she'd be years too early for the next one in 1746. She opened her mouth to screech Rhea's name but shut it abruptly. Alerting the castle guards to her presence was a very bad idea.

She got to her feet, being quiet, and brushed dirt off her pants. Her body felt stiff and bruised, so her fall had been real enough. Her shoulder bag was still with her. Apparently, inanimate objects survived time transits, but she'd found that out the first trip. Kat bit hard on her lower lip. She had to focus, not take mental side trips into inconsequentials.

Who gave a good goddamn if she had her bag? The money wasn't any good, even if she could show herself long enough to spend any of it, which was unlikely.

She felt raw, used. Her little nighttime jaunt took on a whole new meaning. Her sense she hadn't been alone in her hotel room had been spot on, but she wasn't used to paying attention to details like that.

Rhea might have trouble establishing corporeal form in the twenty-first century, but she'd projected enough of herself forward in time to influence Kat's actions.

Why hadn't Arlen warned her?

She bit her lower lip harder, enough to draw blood this time.

None of this was his fault. He wasn't the one with the crazed ancestor. Besides, he'd tried to caution her, but she'd shined him, not taken his concerns seriously enough. He'd said she was vulnerable, but she'd had no idea how defenseless she was.

Kat turned in a slow circle, fully expecting her great-great grandmother to jump out of the murky shadows, but Rhea wasn't there.

"Eleven, and all is well," rang from a parapet far above.

Kat flattened herself against the wall. If they found her, all wouldn't be so fucking well. She was in the same position she'd been in at Inverlochy. If the guard discovered her, they'd assume she was an English spy and execute her summarily. Nothing fancy like juries in this era, particularly not for women.

Because she couldn't come up with a better hiding spot, she made her way to the castle graveyard. It was on the far side, the one not facing the river. As she walked, urging darkness to conceal her, she remembered an earlier version of the burial ground had fronted the River Ness, but it had eroded during a few high-water years, so the remaining crypts and graves had been relocated.

Unlike Inverlochy, she'd never seen anything beyond artist sketches of what earlier versions of this castle looked like. When the graveyard came into view, she was pleased by the presence of crypts. They'd provide a place to hide. She wasn't under any illusions. Come daylight, a woman wearing a zippered jacket and trousers would create havoc.

The metal zipper would be viewed as evidence of deviltry, along with all the electronic devices in her bag. Her trousers would label her as unnatural. The only women who dressed like men were those trying to pass themselves off as such. Ergo: spies.

"Jesus. I am so fucked," she muttered as she picked the largest crypt and peered at the writing over its arched entrance. Not Camerons. Once she established that little fact, she felt her way down a dozen stone steps into the partially buried structure.

The Roskellys had a connection with the Camerons. Maybe if she made a point to stay away from Cameron bones, it would make things harder for Rhea. She shook a fist at the air. Any illusions she'd harbored about her great-great-grandmother's good intentions toward her vanished. Rhea may not be mentally ill by modern definitions, but the old woman was demented in her own way. For her to still be after Kat defied credibility.

Almost thirty years had passed, for chrissakes. Time to give up and move on.

Eh. Maybe time passes differently after you're dead.

Bullshit! I am still making excuses for that woman. I need to stop right now.

She fished in her bag for the penlight she always carried and thumbed it on long enough to examine her surroundings. Rat eyes glowed red from the corners, and the rodents chittered their annoyance at being disturbed.

"Don't get your feathers ruffled." Kat killed the light. No reason to burn up the batteries. She'd seen enough. Her knees felt shaky, so she sank to a marble slab and threaded her fingers through her hair, massaging her aching temples.

There had to be something she could do rather than sit around waiting for inevitable exposure. Someone would find her. Either Rhea or whichever clan was in control of the castle. She tried to recall who'd held the upper hand in the early 1700s but couldn't remember anything beyond the Munros and the Frasers, whose tenure had ended in the middle of the sixteenth century.

Most of the night stretched before her. If she was going to try to save herself, it would be far easier with darkness to mask her movements. She kept rubbing her head, hoping against hope it would spur something other than the desolation running through her.

She sat straighter and clasped her hands together to keep them from shaking. "Let's be methodical," she said quietly and held up an index finger. "I'm probably in the early 1700s just like last time."

She raised a second finger. "I have no idea how to return to my own time."

A third finger. "Which means I'm going to have to trust someone who has enough magic to help me."

A swift, bitter laugh escaped before she cut it off. She'd made a few assumptions, key to which was the existence of magic. Kat shook her head. What the fuck was wrong with her? She'd been dragged backward in time twice—and forward once—and she was still questioning whether magic was real.

It was. It had victimized her.

"For the last time," she hissed. "If Arlen's right and I have my own magic, I'm going to devote every iota of time, attention, and energy to learning it inside and out." She fisted both hands, curling her fingers until nails cut into her palms. She felt like Scarlett O'Hara declaring she'd never be hungry again.

The reference to a fictional event from the 1860s, over a hundred years in the future, made her head spin.

"Focus." She opened her fists, flexing her fingers. If there were ever a situation where she had to play the ball where it lay, this was it.

Her eyes widened. Arlen had said he was older than Rhea. Thomas told her Arlen's family had hailed from Inverness. Putting the two together meant he was here.

Somewhere.

All she had to do was find him.

Or maybe she'd be better served to let him come after her again. How would something like that work? Could two of him exist in the same time or would the presence of the modern version create problems? She let variations of time travel folklore roll through her mind but gave it up as a time-waster. From the *Star Trek* version—where moving so much as a pebble could totally skew the future—to other theories that you could blow up mountains and not alter what was coming down the pike, it was clear no one who'd taken the time to write about it knew jack shit.

Yeah, and the ones who do know have kept conveniently quiet.

Katerina got to her feet. Waiting out the night in

the crypt wasn't wise. Daylight would trap her here, and by the time the following night rolled around, she'd be weaker from no food or water.

The time to leave was now.

Her stomach twisted into a sour knot, but she'd never been one to let fear rule her. She wished she had a general layout for the town, but even if she did, she had no idea how to locate the Druids. She was pretty certain they'd all be together. Safety lay in numbers, and they'd moved from an esteemed position in society to being total outliers.

If the Church found them, they were as good as dead, which argued against them living in Inverness proper.

She snorted. She'd just described her situation to a tee. For some reason, the comparison heartened her, made her feel less alone. Nothing like two hunted entities to support one other. The Church wouldn't spare her any quarter, but neither would the laird's guards.

She walked up the crypt steps and out into the night, but cautiously, checking for the presence of others before she crossed the graveyard. She'd follow the river north toward Moray Firth and the North Sea. Soon, she'd leave the town behind, and hopefully settled lands as well. It might be safe to ask after the

Druids' whereabouts once she was well clear of Inverness.

As she walked, blessing her stout boots and warm clothing, her mind whirled in a million directions. The reason Arlen had found her at Inverlochy was because he'd followed the same path she'd taken. Was moving away from Inverness Castle a mistake on her part?

"Doesn't matter if it is." She was back to muttering out loud. No one was out and about to hear her. Her footsteps were far louder than her voice.

Waiting to be rescued wasn't her style. She'd been delighted when Arlen showed up in the Cameron crypt, but it wasn't his job to risk himself because she'd been a dumbass bitch.

After less than a quarter hour, walls reared before her. Dumbass, indeed. Why had she expected to waltz out of Inverness without tangling with the town gates? They'd be locked until dawn, and she couldn't afford to wait that long. She slunk into an alley that stank of piss even more than the rest of the town and dug into her memory. There had to be a way around the main gates. People came and went at all hours. She knelt and sketched a rough map of a far more contemporary Inverness in the dirt to remind herself where things were. Beauly Firth lay to the west, Moray to the northeast. If she could work her way to the water, she might locate a skiff and circumvent the gate that way.

Perhaps it was part of her heretofore ignored magic, but she'd always been blessed with a decent sense of direction. With it fully deployed, she pushed through an increasingly narrow and winding warren of dirt streets that turned so skinny a horse would have had a hard time navigating them. A couple of times, she chose wrong and backtracked when a path ended abruptly.

Once she came so close to a bum wrapped in rags, she was amazed he didn't waken—until she smelled crudely fermented alcohol and understood he was dead to the world. Kat blessed an era where people took to their beds at night. No one had extra money for fuel to fire lanterns or fireplaces, so the dark hours remained so.

Finally, the footpath she'd chosen led to a rusted trellis. Part of the city wall at a distant point in the past, its staves had been bowed outward by someone hunting for precisely what she sought: a way in and out of Inverness that didn't necessitate being grilled by the gate guards.

Kat didn't question her fortune. She stepped through, thrilled her hunches had worked in her favor. Now all she had to do was keep moving.

And find the Druids.

Exactly how that would happen was anyone's guess, but she'd been lucky so far. No reason her fortune wouldn't hold. She couldn't imagine being stranded in the 1700s forever.

Though the air was damp and promised rain, it held off. She was determined to cover as much ground as she could between now and dawn. One thing bothered her—well more than one, but among the top three was what had happened to Rhea Roskelly?

Her great-great grandmother had dragged her back in time for a reason, presumably to co-opt her into picking up the witch banner. If that was so, where the hell was she?

"Grannie?" Kat kept her voice low.

Rhea didn't answer.

After two more tries, Kat gave up. It was a sure bet if Rhea made her presence known, it would be at the worst possible time. A quarter moon crested the distant horizon but was soon obliterated by clouds. Kat was immersed in thought, developing a probability map of options, when a man materialized out of nowhere and clamped a hand around her upper arm.

She reared back. Reacting instinctively, she screeched, "Let go of me."

"Intriguing, a wench who speaks the English tongue, but oddly."

Crap! Dumbass, once again. She tried to pull away, but it was like attempting to escape a boulder.

The man was swathed in black monk's robes belted

with a leather thong. A hood obscured most of his face. At least he didn't reek as bad as most folk from this era. Between rotting teeth and unwashed flesh, no one smelled very appealing.

Kat cleared her throat and repeated her words in Gaelic as true to the time period as she could muster. "Let go of me."

"I think not, wench. Ye're coming with me."

Panic engulfed her. She twisted and hissed and spit, managing to rake her nails down the man's face before he captured her other hand. A slap landed solidly across her face, followed by a punch to her midsection that made her gasp with pain and knocked the wind out of her. Her face stung, and she sucked air like a gutted fish.

Tears were perilously close to the surface, but she'd be damned if she'd give him the satisfaction of knowing how badly he'd hurt her.

Not just physical damage; her pride had taken a beating too.

This time when he dragged her away from the deserted path along the water, she stumbled after him, cursing herself for a lily-livered coward. If she folded at the first shadow of pain, what chance did she have of surviving?

CHAPTER 8

*A*rlen had been home for a while. He'd poured himself a single malt scotch with the full intention of sitting in front of the fire he'd rustled up with magic, yet he was still pacing up and down his great room. The tumbler was almost empty. He'd never been much for spirits, but worry dogged him.

He'd had the presence of mind to get hold of Sean and the others and let them know not to wait for him. Sean had asked a few questions and received perfunctory replies. Telepathy could be intercepted, so they'd set a time to meet the following morning when it would be safer to talk.

Not only wasn't he a drinking man, he hadn't ever grappled with a woman in his car. His totally-out-of-character spontaneity had to be a byproduct of his magic running up against hers. And the love charm he'd sensed. The one that had nearly been his undoing. She might be magically naïve, but it didn't mean her ability wasn't potent enough to have an effect.

Maybe not just hers, either. Had one of her witchy kin been lurking near enough to try to snare him? If they'd gotten hold of his seed, they could control him. Make his life a living hell.

Despite his dark appraisal, thinking about Katerina made his breath quicken. Arousal spilled through him. While he welcomed the sensations, they worried him too. He shouldn't be reacting to her scent, which still clung to him.

And why not? a dour inner voice demanded.

Arlen shrugged. He was centuries removed from being a randy youth. He'd lived a monkish existence after deciding flings with human women weren't worth it. Their order was small, and all the Druid females mated. Not much magical remained in the twenty-first century, and he'd often wondered why his kind were still around. Their primary function had been keeping evil from interfering with the Earth's natural balance.

Evil remained, but it wasn't the magical variety. Not much those like him could do in the face of atomic weaponry and a warming planet. He ached for Earth. Her days were numbered, her lands overflowing with far too many people, but no one seemed to care.

At least not enough to formulate the kinds of changes that might make a dent in an inevitable slide toward oblivion. He came to a stop next to the scotch. He'd left it out, but when he reached for it, he changed his mind. Liquor wouldn't solve his problems, and he needed a clear head.

Something was going on, something dark and subtle and insidious, but he couldn't quite identify it. He might be overreacting, but he didn't think so. Katerina was a stunning woman, and he was drawn to her in ways he didn't understand. He'd been so aroused by the touch of her lips and body, his mind had checked out. Yet their kiss in the car held elements of coercion simmering in the background.

One thing was certain. If he hadn't interrupted their embrace, they'd have ended up in the miniature backseat with her straddling his lap. Just the thought of her sinking onto his cock, all heat and slickness, almost made him come. He clapped a hand over the tented-out front of his trousers before he realized what he was about.

What? Was he going to drag his dick out in the middle of his living room and shag himself until he came? The way he was feeling, it wouldn't take more than a few strokes.

"Stop it. Just stop." His words were harsh and loud, but they had the desired effect. His arousal receded enough for him to think of something beyond Katerina's high, rounded globes of breasts and the taste of her mouth glued against his as she kissed him. She'd returned his passion with a fire that made him long for her.

He examined his hunger and his need. Both were real enough but tainted with whatever had been skulking on the sidelines since two nights ago in the lecture hall.

He sucked air deep into his lungs, blew it out, and did it again, before standing tall. If he was right, and something evil was creeping about, he'd deal with it immediately. "Show yourself." He added a Gaelic power word to the mix. If anything lurked, it would have no choice but to reveal its presence.

The corners of his vision darkened, and the air took on a decidedly menacing edge. The feel of witch magic pounded him, acrid and sour. Was it Rhea, or was he picking up something from Katerina?

She had the same power as her kinswoman, just no concept what to do with it. Or maybe she wasn't as innocent as she'd led him to believe. He'd assumed her panic in the Cameron crypt was real, but a consummate actress could have faked being scared to her bones.

His arousal scattered, leaving an ache in his balls.

Thank all the gods he hadn't had sex with her. His semen would give her power over him, if she were inclined to grab the upper hand.

Witch power moved toward him from the four corners of the generous great room, creating a gray haze that partially obscured antique furniture, bookcases, and finely crafted art objects he'd collected through his lengthy life. The fire blew out in a whoosh, turning from flames to smoldering cinders.

Arlen squared his shoulders. He'd summoned the thing. He'd see this through. Magic danced to his call, and he draped warding around himself. Before it was complete, he reached for Sean with his mind calling, "*Gabh i leith*." Gaelic for come to me.

Cackling laughter battered him from all sides. He rolled his eyes and said in Gaelic, "If 'tis the most ye can do, best leave off afore ye strain your vocal cords."

He narrowed his eyes, willing the voice to develop a body to go along with it. Sure enough, Rhea took shape out of the misty gloom, flanked by two more witches.

He angled his head. "Dinna care for the odds last time? One on one too much for you?"

"Sling all the shit ye wish," Rhea countered. Her silvery hair shrouded her projection, but enough of her was here for him to do some harm.

"What the unholy fuck?" Another witch with skanky dark hair falling out in patches asked.

"Aye, just our luck," witch number three cut in. "A man who rises above his cock." She dissolved into cackles, maybe at her own play on words about things rising. Her hair had probably been a clear, true red once, but had faded to rust tones splashed with gray.

All three of the women were garbed in tattered black robes. For all he knew, they'd been buried in them.

Arlen cut to the chase. "Lovely of ye three to drop in, but why are ye here?" He eyed the trio. They reminded him of the witches in Macbeth or the Morrigan with her triple nature. Neither analogy made him feel any better.

"We are here," Rhea began, adding a dramatic flourish with both hands. Her nails were cracked with dirt ground beneath them.

"To make certain ye doona interfere a second time," the dark-haired witch clarified.

"Interfere with what?" he asked, projecting confusion. He was quite sure he understood, but keeping them talking meant maybe they wouldn't pay close attention while he cooked up a counter spell to banish them from his home. Besides, if they had information, they might let some of it leak.

Being dead conferred an advantage or two, but it also dulled reasoning ability.

Rhea floated closer, not stopping until her face was only a foot away. She smelled of rot and death with a flowery veneer that didn't do much to mask her stench. "Katerina is mine. I claim her by right of blood. Ye willna interfere."

"Interfere with what?" Arlen shrugged. "As ye can see, I'm here in my home, minding my business. Katerina is her own woman. I left her at her hotel as any gentleman rightly born would have."

"Ye werena so gentlemanly in your car." Rhea's tone was sly.

He buried his reactions deep, along with fervent relief Kat had been a bystander. Rhea was the one on the sidelines orchestrating lust—or feeding the flames since his desire for Kat had a life of its own without help from anyone—living or dead.

"I might have been more forward if I had a taste for ménage a trois." He leered at her. "Or necrophilia."

She hissed, drawing her lips back from yellowed teeth. "Ye upstart."

"I'd watch who ye call names. I'm older than ye lay claim to." He made a dismissive gesture. "I still have no idea why ye're here."

"To make certain ye remain and doona run after our kinswoman as ye did the last time."

Anger did battle with worry. He wanted to tear the witches into untidy pieces—and he might make it through one of them before the others laid into him with teeth, nails, and excoriating magic meant to strip flesh from bones.

It took effort, but he played dumb. "I left her at her hotel. Why would I go after her?"

Rhea snarled, "I canna believe ye're that dense, *Druid*." The way she said Druid made it sound like a curse.

"Fine. Berate a chap for asking an honest question. If 'tis all the same to you, I'd prefer it if ye returned whence ye came. I would retire, and I was serious when I said sex with the dead isn't in my top ten preferred activities."

He gazed from one Roskelly witch to the next and back again. Would they believe his deception? Or would they see right through his flimsy effort for the desperate ploy it was?

The witch with faded red hair sidled close. "Ye only think ye left her at the King's Arms. We had other plans."

Alarm bells tolled, deafening him, but he forced himself to retain a bland demeanor. "Other plans?" He echoed her words. "Like what? Inverness is a wee bit shy on night life."

Another wicked laugh punctuated the spell eddying about him. "Particularly the Inverness where we sent her," the witch retorted.

"Shut up!" Rhea rounded on her. "Just shut up, ye great stupid cow."

"I'll not have ye calling me names." Red hauled off and slapped Rhea, but since neither of them were fully corporeal, the blow bounced off.

Arlen's mind moved with the speed of a riverboat gambler shuffling cards. Goddammit all to hell. Kat must have gone out and been snared in another time-traveling junket. He had to get rid of the dynamic trio, so he could go after her. She wouldn't fare any better in Old Inverness than she would have in Old Ft. William.

He feigned surprise. "Ye went to a lot of trouble to move her backward in time—again. Yet ye're here. Aren't ye a wee bit concerned she'll find a way out of your trickery? After all, she holds the same magic as you."

"Pfft." Rhea spat a thin strand of saliva onto the rug. "If she gets into a dicey spot, she'll welcome me when I show up."

"She's the last of our line," Red piped up.

"I told ye to shut up," Rhea screeched.

Arlen filed the information away. No wonder Rhea was hot on the trail of her great-great granddaughter.

"Let me guess," he said as he let magic seep into him, intent on attacking. "Someone else ye'd counted on either died or defected."

"Died," the black-haired witch snapped. "No one *defects* from the Roskellys. 'Tis an honor to be counted among our number."

Arlen waited through five more seconds before he loosed a volley of power aimed right at Rhea. Her form shattered but regrouped a few feet away. "I thought ye were up to something. Give it up, Druid. Ye're no match for three of us."

"We could lock him in," Red suggested.

"Aye, if we did, then we could follow our kinswoman—ensure her loyalty to us and us alone."

Arlen was done playing with the witches. He fired more power, this time scattering it, so it hit them all. Their bodies barely flickered before shining stronger than ever.

Concern tempered with fury ripped through him. He had to get to Kat before she ran into a rabid churchman. One gander through that shoulder bag she always carried, and she'd be on a one-way trip to the gallows or the pyre. Nothing like an electronic tablet that blinked and beeped and played music to seal your fate.

"Where'd you send her this time?" He tried for authoritative but didn't even fool himself.

"Ye must think we're stupid." Red lifted a corner of her mouth into a sneer.

It took discipline, but he restrained himself from hearty agreement. If he got out of this mess, he could track Kat with magic, so long as her trail hadn't grown too cold.

He glared at the witches. They glared back. Around him, the house grumbled and groaned. Constructed with a generous dollop of Druid magic mixed with Earth power, it resented the witches' presence as much as he did.

Hope flared. The stones and timbers around him could help expel fell energy. He hadn't considered them before, but he did now. The time for elegant and indirect was past. He raised his hands, chanting in ancient Gaelic, the Druids' spell language.

Rhea and her henchwomen laughed, but he kept going. If this worked, they'd be laughing from the stone dungeon, a spot he could hold them with magic once he managed to stuff them inside.

Power rumbled through the stones around him, amplifying his Druid ability beyond his expectations. Power rushed through him; even his voice grew deeper, more commanding. The floor shook; plaster rained down. He could rebuild later. The most important thing was breaking free.

He had to find Kat. And this time, by all the

bloody, fucking saints, he'd teach her magic whether she wanted to learn or not. She had to protect herself or her life would turn into a revolving door as she bounced forward and backward in time. Even if she kept right on telling Rhea to go to hell, eventually, she'd run up against the wrong people, and that would be that.

Blistering insight ran molten, scouring his soul with awareness. She was his. They were fated to be together. Why else would she have been thrust into his path? And he into hers?

Magic called to magic. No two ways to slice it.

With total disregard for his newfound wisdom, the witches uttered blood-curdling cries and threw themselves on him, biting, ripping, tearing with teeth and nails. Christ! They weren't even here, not really, so why was he bleeding from a dozen spots. He tried warding himself, but their magic cut right through his efforts.

When wards didn't work, he slapped and punched and bit back. Grabbing handfuls of hair, he pulled until the witches shrieked with pain, and great hanks of the greasy shit came loose in his hands. He should use magic. It was neater, cleaner, and a whole lot more powerful.

Except, he'd tried it and gotten nowhere. Whatever

he destroyed with Druid magic, they resurrected immediately by applying the darker side of enchantments.

He'd always known black magic was stronger, but when had it outstripped his by such an enormous margin?

When I stopped using magic and lost my touch, he thought sourly and sucker-punched Red in the chest. She opened her mouth and spewed a noxious mix of vomit and saliva all over him. He kicked her from the side and heard ribs breaking. Moaning, she crumpled to the floor and wrapped her arms around herself. Flexible staves shot through the floor, winding themselves around her scrunched up body. She struggled against them, but they held her in place.

Excellent.

He'd been afraid if he hurt the witches too badly, they'd thumb their noses at him and leave. He needed to immobilize them, not have them pop back up like smirking gargoyle targets in a shooting gallery.

One down. Two to go. He could do this. A hunk of plaster the size of a beach ball broke off and fell on Rhea's head, knocking her to her knees. Staves shot out, but before they could snare her, she leapt beyond their reach shouting in a language he'd never heard before.

He'd always suspected black magic practitioners

had their own dialect, but this was the first he'd heard it. He made a point of remembering her words. Maybe there'd be a way to turn witch power against Rhea and the other Roskellys. This batch was the tip of the iceberg. If they failed, others would pick up the slack.

If Katerina was truly the last, they wouldn't rest until she was inculcated into the fold.

A roar rolled through the old house. From the far end, the stout oaken door boomed as it crashed against its stops. Druid energy poured inside, along with their Gaelic war cry rolling from many throats.

Sean, Morgan, and half a dozen others rushed to his side, magic shrouding them and flashing from outstretched hands. He wove his power in with theirs, but in the moments while they joined forces, Rhea and the black-haired Roskelly witch turned into pillars of black-tinged flame and vanished.

"Ye canna leave me," Red wailed from where she thrashed on the floor.

"Ha." Morgan stood over her. "So much for solidarity among witches, eh?" She kicked the witch in her broken ribs.

The witch squealed.

"No time for her," Arlen shouted. "We have to go after Katerina."

"Thought you left her at the King's Arms." Sean was breathing hard, but his immaculately tailored suit was none the worse for his mad dash across Inverness.

"Aye, that I did, but she apparently went out for something—"

"Or was pushed into doing so," Morgan said sourly and gave the witch at her feet another robust kick. "Is that what happened, bitch?"

"A wee suggestion," the witch moaned. "'Twasn't as if we twisted her arm and forced our kinswoman to leave her room."

Arlen hunkered next to the witch. "Where is she?" he thundered.

"Wouldn't ye like to know." Blood dripped from the witch's mouth, staining her chin and teeth.

"Aye, and ye'd like to be free, eh?" He rocked back on his heels, regarding the captive witch.

A shadow crossed her broken face, and she shook her head. "I'd give anything to be free, but the others would kill me."

"I have news, witch," Morgan snarled. "Ye're already dead."

"Look at me." She spat another mouthful of blood, turning the carpet red-black. "Dead doesna mean I canna suffer."

"They left you to rot." Sean joined them.

"Aye, that they did," Arlen agreed. "I'd watch where ye place your loyalties."

The witch turned her face away. Tears slid from beneath her closed lids. When she opened her amber eyes, she said, "Ye'll free me?"

Arlen touched her shoulder, so she'd know he was telling the truth. "We canna afford to waste time picking exit points in the past. If we guess wrong too many times, Katerina will swing from a gibbet afore we arrive."

"Rhea wouldn't allow it." Red sounded indignant.

He didn't point out that being shanghaied into witchcraft wouldn't fly, either. Kat would fight them tooth and nail, but in the end, she'd be just as dead as if a Churchman had found her first.

"Rhea doesn't care as much as all that." Morgan's tone was silk-lined compulsion. "Where is Katerina?"

"1732."

"Inverness, right?" Arlen pressed.

The witch nodded and thrashed weakly. "Free me. We struck a bargain."

"I shall keep my end, but only once I've returned."

"Why ye right bastard," the witch screeched, spraying him with spittle.

He pushed to his feet. "Think about it," he growled. "We free you now, first thing ye'll do is run to Rhea and the other one. Ye'll confess, and they'll move Kat. Unlike ye, I am honorable. Unless ye've destroyed yourself fighting your bonds, I'll sever them as soon as Kat is safely returned."

"I can find her for you." The witch assessed him with shrewd eyes.

"I'll find her on my own, thanks," Arlen retorted. Motioning the Druids to the far side of the room, he draped them in magic to mute their conversation. "Who's coming with me? I'll take two. More than that, and the time-transit magic will become too complex."

"Me," Sean said.

"Aye, and me as well." Morgan screwed her face into a mask that would frighten anyone.

"We'll stand guard over the witch," Will said.

"Aye. In case the two who left have second thoughts and return for her," Krista added. Will's mate, she was just as fair as him. Arlen had always suspected they had faery blood with their white-blonde hair and icy, pale eyes.

"Excellent." Arlen touched both of them briefly on the shoulder.

He thought Rhea and the other witch returning was remote, but it paid to be careful. He let power build around him, as Sean and Morgan threaded their magic with his spell.

Sean held up a hand. "Where are ye aiming for?"

"Where else? Our old stronghold on the banks of Moray Firth."

"Good choice." Morgan's dark eyes flashed silver. "Naught has changed. The Church holds no fondness for us, and we can be killed in any time, not just the current one."

"I have no intention of falling prey to the hangman's noose," Arlen informed her and swept them through a portal that resonated cleanly with his magic. Unlike his last trip through time at the hands of witch power, this journey felt pure, free of taint.

He had one goal. Find Kat and bring her back.

How hard could it be?

He concentrated on his casting. One thing at a time. First, they had to get there. Then, they had to find her. He'd deal with whatever cropped up in between. She was his mate, the woman he'd waited centuries to find...

He ripped the thought out at its roots. She might not view things the same way. In truth, he was certain she wouldn't. One trip through time was a fluke. After her current displacement, she'd catch the first plane back to the U.S. It's what he would do in her place. Besides, why would she relinquish a prestigious academic post to move to Scotland?

He winced. He was getting so far ahead of the game, it was pathetic. He'd be proper and professional. No more stolen kisses. Nothing to bend her to his will.

Except for magic. She'd learn basic defensive maneuvers whether she wished it or not.

The black of his travel spell shaded to gray, and he readied himself to face a much earlier iteration of Inverness. It he'd done this right, they'd come out underground. If he'd screwed things up, they could face anyone from the laird's guard to a group of furious clerics.

Katerina lay on her side in a filthy alcove. Mice squeaked from somewhere close by, but it was too cold for roaches to do much more than waggle their antennae her way. The man who'd nabbed her had dragged her at least a mile to a falling down stone building. It didn't look anything like a church, so her assumption about him being a monk might not be accurate. From his inflection and the guard's "all's well" call, she was spot on about landing in the earlier portion of the 1700s.

Fear carved deep, but now wasn't the time to give in to it. She had to find a way out of her predicament, and she didn't have a whole hell of a lot to work with.

She tried for a more comfortable position, but the maybe-not-a-monk and two others like him had wrapped her in rusty lengths of chain before tossing her into a corner. If she hadn't been the victim, it would have been laughable since none of them wanted to touch her, which was weird since she was clean and they were filthy. At least they hadn't rooted through her bag. It sat in the corner where they'd tossed it. Something about her unnerved them. It wasn't much of an advantage, but it was all she had so far.

They spoke a fractured Latin but were easy enough to understand. She'd held a blank look with downcast eyes to encourage free discourse. Women from this era were almost never educated, so the men assumed she couldn't understand them.

Her deception had worked in her favor; they were chattering like a flock of magpies—as if she weren't even there. At least they hadn't decided to rape her. Not yet, anyway. If that happened, she was pretty sure they'd kill her to conceal their fall from grace. Monks had sex. Lots of it, but they were supposed to be chaste. Even if this group weren't part of one of the "official" religious sects, they dressed as holy men.

"Where'd you find the slut?" one of the men asked. Like the other two, his head was shaven, and he wore a ratty black robe held together with a length of leather.

"Wandering by the river." Her captor lowered his voice. "The wench speaks English."

The other two made hissing noises as if they'd just heard she was the devil incarnate. "What do you suppose she was doing there?" the third man asked. This one's teeth were broken and black.

"No idea."

They crossed the room and circled her, moving close enough she stifled a gag. Damn. People really did stink when they didn't wash frequently. "She's well enough garbed, even if she's dressed up like a man," the one with rotting teeth muttered.

"Mayhap we might ransom her." The other man's dark eyes gleamed hopefully.

"You never were quick on the uptake," the one who'd taken her said. "Who in God's name do you think will own she's theirs?"

"Good enough point," the man agreed. "English, you say?" At the first man's nod, he went on, "Must be a spy."

"Exactly why no one would claim knowledge of her presence here. No upright, God-fearing woman is out and about after dark, either." Her captor nodded sagely, and the men moved back toward the other side of the hovel where a smoky peat fire did almost nothing to warm the place.

She tried to remember what she knew about politics and splinter religious groups from this era. The

Church of Scotland had come to blows with the Calvinists over dogma, the dissention growing more and more bitter and lasting for years. In the 1730s, a series of secessionists formed splinter sects, but she'd be damned if she could recall much about any of them.

Other than they were numerous and not sanctioned by either the Calvinists or the Church of Scotland. Over time the secessionists moved more and more toward evangelism, but it hadn't happened yet.

Crap! One of the men had snatched her bag. It dangled from a grime-crusted fist. The man who'd nabbed her said, "Return that. I found her. Whatever's in there is mine."

The man with the bag didn't make any move to let go of it. "I'd say possession surpasses your claim."

"You would, would you?" Her captor launched himself at the other man and drove him across the room until his back was against the stone wall.

Amid grunting and scrabbling, they traded blows. The third man turned away, ignoring them, and hurried to where she lay. Kat put two and two together about the time he squatted next to her and grabbed a breast. He shoved his other hand between her legs, seemingly flummoxed by her trousers.

She kicked, but he evaded her easily, bound as she was. The hand kneading her breast joined his other one as he hunted for a way into her pants. The other two men were shouting insults in Gaelic as they hit one another. At least her bag had fallen to the floor, no doubt because the man holding it wanted full use of both his fists.

The opportunist who'd thought to rape her while his buddies were otherwise occupied, jumped back as if she'd knifed him in the guts. Kat rolled out of his way, but the wall halted further progress.

What had stymied him? It took a moment before she remembered her zipper. They'd been invented around 1890.

She flipped back around and stared right at him. The time for maidenly modesty was past. She'd scared him, and she'd capitalize on it before he raised the alarm with the other two still duking it out over first dibs on her bag. The pervert loomed over her, dark eyes rimmed with white, but the front of his robes stuck out, so fear hadn't deflated his erection.

Pasting a come-hither look on her face, she took a chance and smiled fetchingly. "Come on back, here," she invited in Gaelic. "No one will notice."

He took a step away from her and made the hooked finger sign against evil. "Ye're a witch," he snarled.

Kat shrugged. "So? Everyone is something."

The white rims around his pupils grew larger. "Abomination. My seed will turn me to your bidding."

Kat lowered her voice. "But ye knew that when ye

came over here. Untie me. Ye willna be sorry. I can show ye things that will spoil ye for any other woman."

He cupped a hand over his erection. He was frightened of her, but she fascinated him too. Would lust win out?

The man who'd snagged her staggered to them. "What the fuck is going on over here, eh? Riley? Answer me." He slugged the one who'd been freaked out by her zipper in the kidneys.

Riley grunted, but didn't fall forward. Good thing. He'd have fallen right on top of her. She adopted her diffident expression, gaze averted, and held her breath. Would Riley admit what he'd been about and start jabbering about her zipper? He wouldn't have a name for it, but that didn't matter.

After a sullen glance at the other man, Riley remained silent.

It made sense. Sex wasn't a prime discussion topic among those who donned religious robes. The banter about wenches with pox she'd overhead outside Inverlochy Castle would never have happened inside a monastery.

Her captor doubled up his fist again. Before he could slam it into Riley a second time, the man sidestepped him. "Naught. There's naught happening here." Ducking, he slipped through what was left of the half fallen-in stone archway that served as a door.

Kat felt her captor's gaze staring down at her, sharp with speculation. He'd likely overheard some of her conversation with Riley. In a lightning-fast move, he bent and slapped her. Her head snapped back, and her cheek stung.

"I bound ye with iron. It should mute your magic, witch."

She narrowed her eyes and stared back at him, wishing she had the power he assumed she held.

"What did ye do to Riley?" He prodded her in the side with a boot, avoiding her direct gaze.

The other man crawled to them before rising creakily to his feet, the earlier altercation apparently forgotten. Such events were commonplace in this era, barely worth notice. He hooked a hand around her kidnaper's upper arm. "Don't engage her in conversation," he instructed in Latin.

"Probably wise," her captor replied in kind and turned away.

Breath rattled from Kat. How had she ever thought she'd outsmart these bastards? Not that they were mental giants, but she was trapped. Vulnerable to their whims. Her bag mocked her from where it had fallen onto the uneven dirt floor. Once they got they paws into it, Riley's horror at her zipper would fade to nothing compared with the men's reaction to her phone and tablet.

Assuming they could figure out which buttons turned them on.

Or her wallet and passport complete with credit cards and likenesses of her. Cameras were at least a hundred years away. No way to explain the nice, neat photographs on her driver's license or passport.

Kat cringed.

Of course, there was a way. Witchcraft. She could almost see them building a pyre out behind the building and tossing her onto it just before they lit the tinder.

"Come on." The man who'd lost the fight angled his chin at the door and walked through it after Riley.

After one long, penetrating glance her way, the man who'd ruined her plans—and maybe her life— followed the other one, leaving her alone. She snorted. Not much of a risk. They assumed iron would keep her magic contained. They had no idea of the truth.

If they did, they'd have murdered her on the spot. Time travel was impossible, which made her presence in this crumbling shepherd's hovel equally impossible. Men like the ones milling about somewhere outside were scarcely philosophers. Anything that flew in the face of their beliefs had to be snuffed out.

She wriggled, trying to find a way out of her bonds. The men had been sloppy, but even slop didn't leave much space for escaping metal rings. She didn't care for her thoughts. They were defeatist, and she had to boot them out of her head.

Defeat had never been part of her vocabulary, and she'd be goddamned if she'd add it now.

She thought about Arlen and hoped to hell he wouldn't gallop after her like an avenging angel. If anything happened to him because of her stupidity, she'd have a hell of a hard time coming to terms with it.

He'd been convinced she had magic.

Okay.

Time to accept it. Granted, she was untrained, but everyone had to start somewhere. She shut her eyes and imagined one of the iron rings snapping. She visualized it, concepted it, pushed for it. The links actually rattled against each other, but nothing else happened.

"I made them clatter," she muttered. "Got to try harder."

Folklore from the time said iron would bind witches, but her research suggested true binding elements came from the natural world. From earth and stone and wood. None of them were in play. She squeezed her eyes tight and focused on a single link. A particularly rusty one in the chain around her ankles.

It rocked and twisted.

Kat dug deeper, giving it everything she had. She was breathing hard now; sweat slicked her sides and forehead, despite how cold it was. If the men returned, she was screwed. They'd add more lengths of chain to those already circling her. At least a display of power might keep their dicks beneath their robes, but it wouldn't keep them from immolating her.

She glommed onto the display of power thought, forcing herself to believe she could do this. Faith in outcomes was the key to everything else, so it probably worked for magic as well. Her temples throbbed, and she gasped air through the narrow place her throat had become. The link heated, burning her skin, but she pushed harder.

With a small, discreet clink—no fanfare at all —it broke.

Unbelieving, Kat stared at it. Still glowing red, it lay in the dirt. Hurrying, she unwound the chain from her ankles. The only length remaining spanned her back and looped around her wrists. Angling her head, she listened carefully but didn't hear the hum of conversation.

Either the men weren't talking, or they'd gone a distance from the building. She hoped for the latter and focused her attention on another weak, rusty link. Maybe because she'd already done it once, this time her efforts paid off much faster and the chain slithered away from her body, creating a pile on the floor.

Free. I'm free.

She started to get up, but daylight was leaching through cracks between the stones. Her chances of escape were almost nil. All the trees in the Highlands had been chopped down for buildings or fuel long since. Nothing provided much in the way of cover.

Her bag still lay where the men had dropped it. She crawled to it and dragged it next to her. Daylight or not, she had to make a run for it. Waiting for the men to return was tantamount to a death sentence. Who knew what they were hatching up? For all she knew, they planned to sell her to a local sorcerer. Women were chattel, not to be bothered with.

She'd turned into more trouble than they bargained for, and them plotting to rid themselves of her for profit made sense.

Arlen marched across her mind. If she ever found her way back, she'd take him up on his offer to shepherd her power into something usable. Something she understood. The memory of his mouth on hers made her smile. He was such a gorgeous man, but he'd never want her. She was forthright, pushy, and outspoken, nothing like the well-mannered women he probably valued.

He'd been furious when he'd shown up in 1700s

Inverlochy. Livid at her for not paying attention to his instructions. For giving him the slip when all he'd been trying to do was help her. He'd known something was up with her and sensed how unnerved she was that night in the lecture hall. His offer of lunch and a tour of Inverness took on a whole new dimension, and she kicked herself for misinterpreting his intentions.

She owed him a major apology, something far more believable than the paltry pretense she'd paid lip service to.

Thomas as well. He'd tried to hold her back from making a huge mistake and gotten shit for his troubles.

Crap. All I seem to be doing is leaving a string of things I'm sorry for. I need to start thinking before I leap.

No time like the present to leave the dank, smoky pit of a shack. It had no windows, so she had to reveal her freedom to take a peek out the door. Not that she couldn't have shuffled over there, shackles and all, but they'd have made it impossible for her to run.

Dawn was breaking. In northern Scotland in the dead of winter, it meant the black of night was yielding to gray, and it was like as not around ten thirty. She listened intently but didn't hear anything beyond the cries of raptors on the hunt for rodents that were late returning to their dens.

The men were nowhere in sight.

She slipped her bag over one shoulder. If it didn't contain such damning evidence, she'd just leave the thing behind. Should she return the way she'd come? Or head south into open country? If she traveled south, she could circle back to Inverness. Maybe if she returned to the castle, she could reverse the enchantment that had dragged her backward in time.

It was worth a shot. She'd summoned enough power to break the iron links. If she could do that, maybe she could make it back to where she'd started. Arlen had mentioned Rhea had an affinity for the time period she'd been born into. If it worked for her great-great grannie, maybe the same would hold true for her.

Feeling naked and exposed, Kat set out. After she'd put a hundred yards between herself and the hut, she felt better. The land was littered with boulders, some large enough to hide behind.

Eventually, the men would return. Would they track her? She stared at her boot prints, clearly visible in the perpetually wet dirt. Nothing like leaving a trail screaming, "Kat went this way." Should she make an attempt to obliterate evidence of her passage?

No. It would take too long, and she'd be damned if she'd backtrack. Speed was her friend, so she kept moving. Rain first threatened and then fell in huge, heavy drops from the cloudy, gray sky. She pulled her hood over her head and yanked the zipper to her chin.

Lightning crackled, followed by the ominous boom of thunder.

What the fuck? Electrical storms weren't common in the early morning. The air thickened around her, developing the same feel the crypt behind Inverlochy's ruins had held.

Kat halted, staring into the gloom. Goddammit! She'd wondered where Rhea was when she first ended up here. *Yeah, and I told myself she'd show up at the worst possible time, and voila, here she is.*

"For fuck's sake, show yourself," Kat growled, not in the mood for an arcane game of cat and mouse.

A flickering gateway formed. Rhea stepped through accompanied by a woman with dark hair. Presumably another of her dead kinswomen. "Ye've led me on a merry chase," Rhea said without preamble. "Why canna ye stay put?"

"Because I have a nasty habit of resenting being manipulated." Kat crossed her arms beneath her breasts. "I demand you return me to my own time. Immediately."

"Oh, ye demand it, do ye?" Gales of laughter rolled from Rhea and the other shade.

"Who the fuck are you?" Kat demanded and walked close enough to thump the other woman in the chest with an index finger. It almost penetrated, but not quite.

"That's no way to speak to your great-aunt," the witch sputtered.

"Aye. Show some respect," Rhea chimed in.

"Why?" Kat countered. "You haven't respected me at all." She stalked as close to Rhea as she could get, noticing her great-great grandmother's ghost hovered an inch or two above the ground.

Before Rhea could respond, she continued. "Hear me loud and clear. I have zero interest in being conscripted into witch-hood. None. I will fight you at every turn. I'd rather be dead than be like you."

A shocked look blossomed on Rhea's face. "Ye doona mean that, great-great-granddaughter."

"Yeah, I do. You would have turned me to your will when I was too young to understand—or protest. Mom and Grannie viewed you as such a big threat, they committed you. I have no idea how they pulled the strings to accomplish it. For all I know, they used magic to bamboozle a judge. They loved me. You only love wielding black magic."

Kat's chest tightened. She was chopping through ties she'd clung to since childhood, but she had to be ruthless or Rhea would sense a chink in her resolve and exploit it.

"Ye dinna tell me how much she hates you," her aunt said to Rhea, sounding surprised.

"She never used to hate me." Rhea's tone held

censure, and she turned an injured expression Kat's way. "We can move past this, great-great granddaughter. Ye've misinterpreted things."

Warm, syrupy magic flowed over Kat. Everything would be all right. Rhea loved her after all. Her mother and grannie had things wrong. They'd given her a bum steer, but all was forgiven—

"Stop it," she snarled.

"Stop what, dear?" Rhea asked.

"You're using magic to manipulate me. It won't work."

"How can it not work, child?" her great-aunt asked. "Ye're a Roskelly, same as the rest of us. We need living blood to ensure our line doesna die out. Ye're young, healthy. Ye could produce bairns—"

"I think not," Kat interrupted, not caring she was being rude. "If you believe I'm going to serve as a broodmare so your brand of evil is perpetuated, you're delusional." She stood tall. "This conversation is over."

Kat tried to turn away but couldn't move. Her limbs were locked in place.

"I think not." Rhea threw Kat's words back in her face. "Our conversation has barely begun. Ye will heed my words and comply."

"She's this way," a man's voice rang out, speaking Latin.

Kat tried to look in the direction the voice was

coming from, but her paralysis was absolute. Fuck! Could things get any worse? The men from earlier had tracked her. No doubt they'd brokered some cushy deal with her as an inducement.

Rhea and Great-Aunt No Name turned as a unit, chanting in a language Kat had never heard before. Heavy on consonants, it sounded like a perversion of German.

The three men came into view, running full out. Behind them was a fourth wearing black vestments, complete with a heavy gold cross suspended from a silver chain. The cross was set with three red gemstones that glowed as if lit from within.

"Oooh, fun," Rhea crooned.

"Four holy men." Aunt No Name rubbed her hands together and raised them. Black-tinged power flashed from her outstretched fingers.

Rhea blasted the men from where she stood next to Auntie. The ones from the cabin clutched their chests and fell to the wet ground, writhing in agony. The priest stepped back a pace, hands clutched around the crucifix, chanting in Latin. Power jetted from him. Glistening white threads ran up against witch enchantment creating miniature explosions where the two collided.

The beat of horse hooves moved toward them. Lots of horses, which probably meant reinforcements for the priest. Or it might mean the local laird was sending reinforcements. Either way, it wasn't good.

Kat picked up an experimental foot, surprised she could move. Apparently, magic only went so far, and the stuff that had bound her had been redirected. She'd be goddamned if she'd wait around for her kinswomen to snare her again. To prevent it happening, she took off at a dead run, bag thumping against her side.

Rhea and Aunt No Name could find her. They'd track her through blood ties, but she wouldn't make it easy for them. She uttered a prayer for the priest and whoever was on their way to help him. Maybe he'd keep the witches busy long enough for her to get away.

As she ran, slogging through puddles and slick, slippery mud, she opened herself, heart, mind, and soul, to Arlen. She was done being strong. If he heard her and came for her, she'd be in his debt forever.

If he didn't show up, she'd keep on doing her damnedest to untangle the mess she'd made. Escaping from the eighteenth century hurtled to the tiptop of her list. She didn't belong here. Any fantasies she'd spun about doing research in prima facie territory went up in smoke.

A bitter laugh rolled through her mind at all the podiums she'd stood on, extolling her knowledge of the 1700s. She might have been privy to a few facts, but she hadn't had any idea what things were really like, and she still didn't.

Kat ran raster, altering course to intercept the town wall looming to her right. Humility wasn't a bad thing. She snorted and hoped to hell her slice of humble pie hadn't been carved too small and arrived too late.

$\mathcal{A}$rlen called a mage light and examined the place they'd landed. It was their old cave, but the entrance end had fallen in.

"Win some, lose some," Sean said, sounding far too cheerful.

"I can fix this." Morgan ran lightly to the rockfall. Power jumped from her fingertips, and a path opened for them, amid noisy scraping as stones moved aside. She dusted her hands together and sprinted across the rubble.

Arlen almost fell over her where she'd stopped at what used to be a well-hidden entry point. "Hush." She angled a look at both men.

Arlen sent a thread of seeking magic snaking outward. What reached him was so unbelievable, he repeated his actions. With the same result.

"Hunters?" Sean barely breathed the word into Arlen's mind.

Morgan hissed in frustration.

"'Tisn't possible. They all died out in the Middle Ages." Arlen kept his voice very low.

"Not all of them," Morgan whispered back. "I sense at least six, maybe a few more than that."

"Probably safer not to use telepathy," Sean mumbled sourly.

Arlen agreed. Hunters had magic, often not much, but magic sang to its own. The Church dressed them as clerics and commissioned them to seek out every other entity with power and wipe them out. Although they were an equal opportunity destroyer, they'd focused most of their efforts on witches. Somewhere in the 1400s, a wizard had crafted gemstones that glowed in the presence of witch power. Made it far easier to locate and annihilate them.

"Goddammit!" He clapped a hand over his mouth and lowered his voice. "Do you suppose they're after Kat?"

"Her or her witchy kin." Sean nodded grimly.

A shriek, raw, untamed, not titrated at all, roared through Arlen's mind. Kat was screaming for him.

Screaming loud enough for every Hunter in a million-kilometer radius to pick up on her sending.

"Oberon's balls, man." Sean gripped Arlen's arm. "Can you shut her up?"

"I can try."

Arlen focused his mind voice, narrowing it to a funnel meant just for Kat. *"Hush, darling. I'm close, but you must be silent. Fell things are afoot, and for once 'tisn't your relatives."*

He waited through the space between three breaths, but she must have heard him because the frantic sending that held his name wasn't repeated. Either she'd heard him, or the Hunters had nabbed her.

The thought sent ice chips scudding through his blood. Hunters kept themselves going by cutting power out of those who had it and feeding themselves. The process was bloody and excruciating since the victims were still alive while Hunters drained them. Kat's magic would appear very attractive since Rhea and the other witch were already dead.

Arlen ground his teeth. He was assuming the dead Roskelly duo had shown up here, but it was almost a given. The witches had gone to a lot of trouble to move Kat to this locale. And they'd left Arlen's in one hell of a hurry.

"Katerina is this way." Arlen set off at a magic-fueled lope flanked by Sean and Morgan. What would they find? Maybe he'd been shortsighted not bringing more of them, but then he realized plenty of Druids were already here. All he needed to do was put out the call.

It would mean he'd run up against his two-hundred-years-ago self, but that wasn't a problem. They could coexist for a short time before the warp and weft of time ejected him. "Do we need help?" he asked.

"Let's wait and see what we face," Sean replied.

"Aye, mayhap we'll catch a break." Morgan's beauty had turned harsh and foreboding. She braided her silvery hair out of the way as she ran.

Arlen held a sense of Kat's energy. He'd glommed onto it when her frantic cries reached him. They were almost to Inverness's town walls when he skidded into a declination beneath two enormous stones. Once standing monoliths, they'd fallen against one another, forming a rough vee.

Kat huddled beneath them, her face white and strained.

Arlen wanted to gather her into his arms and never let go. Instead, he nodded curtly. "Come on, lass. We have to leave."

She crept from her hiding place, her usual confident demeanor absent. "I'm sorry."

"Be sorry later," Sean muttered.

Arlen heard horses bearing down on them. He pulled power as hard and as fast as he could.

Didn't matter who was coming, it couldn't be good.

Kat's head snapped in that direction. "Damn it. They have to be the same ones. They're the only horses I've heard since I got here. Must mean they're done with Rhea and Auntie."

"Who's they?" Sean asked.

"There was a priest. Before I ran from him, I heard horses and figured reinforcements were on their way."

"Awk. You've seen Hunters." Morgan grasped Kat's arm.

"Huh? I saw a priest is all."

"Aye, but was his cross set with glowing gems?"

Kat nodded. "Yeah, but how could you possibly know that?"

"No time for explanations," Morgan said. "I have to help Arlen, or none of us will escape."

Arlen felt Sean and Morgan open channels to their magic. He drew on it shamelessly and visualized his manor house. The spell bubbled and boiled around the four of them but didn't take off. Inverness's walls refused to vanish. Worse, a phalanx of priests in black cassocks galloped toward them. Every single one clutched a cross with gems embedded in the gold.

Rubies, sapphires, and emeralds glowed hotly with an unnatural light.

"Redirect!" Sean yelled.

"Aye. We must fight," Morgan bellowed.

Arlen threw his mind voice wide open, summoning Druids to their aid. The earth heard his plea. A rolling quake started in front of the first horseman, unseating him. The other horses peeled off to one side or another, so at least the mini-earthquake was a deterrent.

It bought them a few moments, not much more than that.

Arlen extended his arm and directed lethal magic at the fallen man. A lightning bolt caught the priest's robes, and the man turned into a smoking pyre, squealing in agony as enchanted flames ate him alive. Killing was scarcely second nature for Druids, but Arlen had done plenty in his time.

Hunters deserved death, and he waited for another of the bastards to come close enough to target.

Kat watched him, wide-eyed. Her rain-wet hair clung to her face in sodden clumps. She hadn't said a word, but she didn't have to. Disgust and revulsion rolled off her. He felt like shaking her and screeching, "Ye doona like this? Ye should have remained in your room, not gone wandering about in the dead of night when magic is most powerful."

The horses were circling, their riders intent on catching Arlen's small group from behind, but Arlen was ready for them. So were Sean and Morgan. They'd killed two more of the black-robed horrors when a glowing portal formed fifty yards away. Druids poured through the opening with a cloud of glistening light surrounding them. Emotion buffeted Arlen. Gratitude toward his people. Worry they'd outed themselves sufficiently, they'd become even bigger targets than they already were.

"Thank you," he shouted.

"Doona mention it. We always did love a good scrap."

The early version of him shoved a fist skyward and launched himself at a rider, unseating him and pinning him to the ground. A quick grab freed the priest's lance, and Arlen's double jammed it through the holy man's throat. Blood geysered, and he pushed off his prey. As he balanced on the balls of his feet, gaze sharp and ready, Arlen knew exactly what his earlier self was thinking.

Bring it on.

He'd been there. Killing evil was a high like no other, and he missed the challenge and the rush.

The four riders who remained, charged as a unit. They knew they were dead men, but they were fighting for the glory of God. Death was a small price to pay for an eternal seat in a mythical kingdom that didn't exist.

Arlen laughed. Grim, harsh, bitter. Men were such fools. Manipulated by dreams of glory and the hype of a life after this one that would be better. He joined his earlier self, and together they killed another priest. The field stank of blood and spilled entrails. Crows were gathering. Delighted by the unexpected feast, they whirled in flocks cawing encouragement from overhead.

The two priests who remained must have suddenly decided the price was too high, or the odds too low. Wheeling, they galloped toward Moray Firth, no doubt headed back to report the disaster to the Church of Scotland.

The Druids hadn't bothered to close their portal, and they eddied toward it, a magical tide flowing away, except for four who used power to draw a few of the riderless horses back toward where they stood. The livestock were unexpected bounty, and the Druids wouldn't bypass an opportunity to filch them.

Arlen was proud of his people. He'd run a tight ship back in the day. The twenty-first century had made him sloppy, but he aimed to correct his shortcomings at the earliest opportunity.

1700s Arlen vaulted atop a bay stallion and placed a closed fist over his heart. The other three Druids, also on horseback, rode toward him. Two more loose horses trotted along.

Arlen returned the closed fist gesture. Jagged vibrations pierced him as the future beckoned. He'd overstayed his welcome. So had Sean and Morgan. Only one of them was allowed at a time.

"Time to go." He whistled as loud as he could.

Kat huddled next to him, still looking shell-shocked. Morgan and Sean ran to his side. Redirecting the power eddying about them, they wove it into his time transit casting.

The air warmed with magic, pricking his skin and filling his nostrils with the clean, fresh scent of Druid power. Unlike witches, their magic carried the smells of earth and greenery, of stones washed by rushing rivers. The town walls vanished, replaced by blackness.

An arm wove around him. Kat. She was shaking, and he held onto her, determined to see her back safely. No matter how tough she thought she was, she'd come from a battle. Nothing ever prepared you for seeing a man die in front of you for the first time.

Or the second.

Or the third.

His great room shimmered into being, and they rolled out onto its thick rugs. Will and Krista sat next to the witch. Her nostrils twitched, and she opened eyes the shade of aged whiskey.

"You," she hissed. "Naught but trouble."

Kat didn't bother to reply. She swayed on her feet, and Arlen led her to a chair and pushed her into it.

"Hang on," he said and made a quick trip to the wet bar, returning with a tumblerful of whiskey.

She grasped it with both hands and took enough of a swallow to make her gasp as the fiery liquid ran down her throat. Setting the glass down with a clank, she said, "Before I lose my resolve." She swallowed more liquor. "You said you'd teach me about my magic. I have to do that. No fucking way am I going to get shanghaied into the past every time Rhea gets a wild hair up her ass."

"Speaking of her, where is your kinswoman?" Morgan selected a bottle of mead. Not bothering with a glass, she upended it, drinking deeply.

"I don't know. I ran when the first priest showed up, except he wasn't on a horse. Same cross though. With the eerie gems that look like eyes."

"My sisters are back in their crypts," the red-haired witch said dully, followed by, "Ye promised to release me."

"So I did." Arlen sent magic skittering across the great room, and the staves holding her snapped into pieces.

The witch jumped to her feet, chanting crazily. Moments later, she'd vanished.

"You could have at least thanked me," Arlen called after her.

"Eh, her kind doesn't know the meaning of thanks," Will retorted and made a face.

"Wonder which Roskelly she was," Kat mumbled and drank more whiskey.

"Does it matter?" Morgan asked.

Kat rolled her eyes. "No. Don't mind me. I'm not exactly all here. Except I am here and not there, which makes all the difference in the world. And I'm not making any sense at all." Her eyes filled with tears. "Thank all of you so much. I'm indebted to you forever. I was stupid, filled with hubris, sure I knew better than any of you what was right. Jesus, how could I have been such a dolt?"

She set the glass down, dropped her head into her hands, and sobbed.

Arlen couldn't stand it. He went to her and knelt by her side, placing his arms around her. She didn't pull away, and it gave him hope she didn't hate the feral, untamed part of him that had come out to play killing priests.

"Probably a good time for us to leave," Sean said.

"Aye, but we'll want a full report come the morrow," Will and Krista said almost in unison.

"A full report, indeed," Morgan seconded.

The great room was already flooded with Druid power. It thickened still more, and then he was alone with Katerina crying in his arms.

"We need to talk," he said, keeping his voice soothing, "but it doesn't have to be today."

She lifted her tear-stained face from his chest. "Yes, it does. I'll never sleep if I don't tell someone." Her eyes darkened with horror at the things she'd seen. "I may never sleep again anyway, but at least if I talk with you, I'll have a fighting chance."

"Take your time." He settled in next to her and sent a thread of magic to retrieve the whiskey bottle. It floated across the room, and he snatched it out of the air.

"That's a neat trick." She tried to smile but couldn't pull it off.

"I'll teach it to you."

"Thanks. I was afraid you'd be so furious with me you'd never talk with me again."

"Close." He smoothed hair back from her face.

"But no cigar?" She angled a red brow.

"Och. You Americans and your aphorisms."

He waited as she told him about her evening in fits and starts, from when she'd struck on going out for a ramble as the way to soothe her mental unrest.

"Except, it wasn't me at all," she said, "but Rhea who needed me outside the hotel, so she could drag me backward in time."

"Good you recognize it, lass, now go on."

He snarled when she got to the part about the perverted monk.

"What was he?" she demanded. "I thought maybe some religious splinter group since they were living in a decrepit stone hut."

"Could be a lot of things," Arlen replied. "The secessionists were just getting going then, but you're right they weren't Calvinists or part of the Church of Scotland. If they were, they'd have had better cassocks and not been living so far away from the church proper."

Fear for her cut deep. It was a miracle she hadn't been raped and then killed. When she relayed how she'd focused magic to cut through her chains, pride filled him. "Mayhap, you don't need me as much as you think you do," he said quietly.

She leaned into him. "But I do. If I'm ever in a bad place again, I don't want to be questing about using trial and error."

He didn't tell her that sometimes trial and error was the best he could do. Magic was a fickle bitch, and she often responded differently predicated on a whole lot of uncontrolled variables.

After relaying the next part where she'd run from the hut and met up with both her kinswomen, the first priest, and her original captors, she asked, "What were those glowing stones?"

Arlen had been waiting for that question, but he hadn't settled on how to answer her.

"Truth." She lifted her chin.

He shut his eyes for a moment before snaring her gaze and holding it. "Men with those gems are Hunters. Morgan told you that much. The Church employed them to run down those with magic and kill them. Hunters have power of their own, but the Church allowed it because they were useful."

"They'd have killed me."

He nodded. "The stones burn brightest for witches. They were created by a long-ago sorcerer who hated them."

She angled her head to one side. "You left something out."

It was the second time she'd done that to him, used her magic to intuit something was missing. "Aye. What I skipped over is how they kill other magic-wielders. They gut you in such a way they can feast on your power, using it to strengthen their own."

"Ewww." She made a face. "Like vampires."

"Aye, lass. Very much like vampires. Except when Hunters are done with you, you remain dead."

"No returning as a junior-grade Hunter?"

"Nay."

She sat straighter and raked hair back from her face. "Nothing more to tell. I screamed for you, and you answered me, so I went to ground the first spot I saw."

"The standing stones were a good shelter. Even fallen as those two were, they contained power in their own right."

"Rhea isn't done with me. She'll try again." Kat's voice shook, but strength shone from her eyes.

"She left you alone for years." Arlen tried for soothing. The lass had been through so much, now wasn't the time to mention she was the Roskellys' last hope for continuation of their line.

Kat closed her teeth over her lower lip. "Sorry. I failed to mention this, but I figure I'm the last of them, and they need me to produce more witchy spawn."

Arlen nodded.

Kat narrowed her eyes. "Does that chin shake mean you knew?"

"Aye, lass, but we don't have to—"

"Oh yes, we do." Her expression turned even more somber. "We need to begin those magic lessons right away." Her pale cheeks splotched with color, and she added, "So long as you have time to work me in. I understand you probably have a full work schedule and—"

"What about your schedule?" he cut in.

"Oh yes. That." She squeezed her eyes shut before opening them. "I'm too tired to go there."

"You have every right to be tired. It's early afternoon, and you didn't get any sleep last night."

Kat stumbled to her feet. Crossing the room, she grabbed her bag and dug through it, coming up with her phone. She waved it in his direction. "Never thought just seeing a Verizon logo would make me happy."

He stood too and walked to where she stood. "What are you doing?"

"Calling a cab. What else? I need to get back to the hotel before I fall on my face."

He squelched a smile. "Last time it was pitch facedown into your soup."

"Same thing." She shrugged and tapped the phone display.

Arlen placed a hand across the screen. He didn't want to come off as overbearing, but nor did he want her to leave. He couldn't protect her nearly as well if she put distance between them.

For once, words eluded him. She pushed at his hand and looked at him, a quizzical expression on her face.

"Doona take this wrong." He winced. For some reason, he'd retreated to Gaelic.

Her quizzical expression turned pointed, and she looked more like the strong-willed, abrasive professor who'd made her mark researching the clans. "Doona take what wrong?" She matched his Gaelic, and he blessed her facility with languages.

He spread his arms in an expansive gesture. "This is a big house. Lots of unused bedrooms. Please. I'd consider it an honor if ye'd remain here."

Her testy expression softened. "Thanks. I didn't really want to leave, but I didn't want to intrude where I don't belong, either. The hotel's paid for, and—"

Arlen laid two fingers over her mouth. He was being terribly forward, but he'd apologize later. "Hush." A corner of his mouth twisted downward. "I went to a lot of trouble rescuing you—twice. Least ye can do is let a chap keep a close eye on you."

She closed her teeth over her lower lip and reverted to English. "Is there some way to bar Rhea from this house?"

He wanted to lie so she'd sleep better, but he couldn't do that to her. "Not really. Until ye strengthen your innate power, she'll keep trying. Mayhap even afterward, but ye're stronger than she is."

"No, I'm not. At least, not yet."

"Aye, lassie. Ye're alive. It gives you an edge."

"You're just trying to make me feel better. Before, you said being dead conferred advantages. You can't have it both ways."

"The only plus your kinswoman has—and 'tis

significant—is we canna banish her. No matter what we do, she can find ways to return."

"Until she gives up." Determination ran beneath Kat's words. "I can out-stubborn her."

Arlen had moved his hand from her face to her shoulder. He squeezed gently, loving how she felt beneath his touch, all fluid skin and muscle stretched over bones. Desire kindled. He wanted to sweep her into his arms and carry her upstairs.

She leaned into his touch, swaying on her feet from weariness. Guilt needled him. The lass needed food, rest, mayhap a hot bath to help her relax. Beyond that, he was filthy, his clothes and skin streaked with dried blood and dirt. He moved his fingers from her shoulder down her arm until she laced her fingers with his.

Holding her hand, he led the way upstairs. He'd offer her the chamber right next to his. That way, he could keep the inner door open and watch over her while she slept.

What he wanted was to watch over her forever, but she had to come to him on her own, not because she was frightened or exhausted or wrung out. And certainly not because her witchy ancestor was hanging about in the wings pushing for them to have sex. Thinking about Rhea infuriated him. If she weren't already dead, he'd have enjoyed ending her life.

They'd reached the third-floor landing, and Kat

looked sidelong at him. "You're angry. If you've rethought me staying here—"

He didn't question her perceptions. They were part of how her magic worked. Arlen swung her to face him. "Not angry with you. How could I be?"

She turned the hand he wasn't holding palm up. "Because I'm pigheaded and don't follow instructions very well."

He skipped the observation about her knowing herself quite well, and said, "I find those traits refreshing, appealing—"

Before he got any more words out, she threw her arms around his neck, stretched onto tiptoe, and kissed him, sweet, hard, and quick. When she lifted her mouth from his, she said, "It's just me here in this hallway. Rhea isn't anywhere around. You've turned me down twice, Arlen MacGregor. Send me away a third time, and I'll never trouble you again."

Emotion thickened his throat. Not trusting himself to speak, he wrapped her in his arms and crushed his mouth over hers.

CHAPTER 11

Short Time Earlier

Between talking about what she'd lived through and the tumbler of hooch, Kat felt more like herself than she had since she'd landed in Old Inverness, beyond the reach of her own time. Some parts of her story were harder than others. She still felt dirty remembering the faux-holy man, his eyes burning with lust as he pawed at her.

Arlen was a good listener. Quiet and patient, he asked questions but didn't drag the story out of her faster than she wanted to tell it. His support went a long way to help her put events in perspective, as did his approval of how she'd handled things.

Maybe he was restraining himself, but he hadn't rebuked her for leaving her hotel in the first place. He had probed, but gently, drawing out her reactions to watching him kill the Hunters. She'd been honest about the mixture of revulsion and fierceness that had confused her at first. Until she recognized he'd done what he did to protect her—and the other Druids...

"Latin?" he asked.

Immersed in thought, she'd missed the first part of his question. "Sorry, what about Latin?"

"I was wondering if you speak Greek as well?"

"Um, yeah. Sumerian too, and I can decode Linear A and B."

He rolled his eyes. "Why am I not surprised?"

"I bet you know them as well."

"Aye, that I do, but our educational system is more slanted toward antiquities."

Much as she wanted to launch a defense of U.S. universities, his observation was true. She stole a sidelong glance at him. Such a beautiful man. Blunt-cut dark hair fell across his face, brushing his shoulders. He must want to change his clothes, yet he hadn't left her side. Dirt-streaked and bloody, speckled with singe marks, his trousers, shirt, and jacket still showcased his broad-shouldered build.

Thinking about him changing reminded her she needed to leave, and she got up intent on her bag and phone. She'd call a cab, and maybe they could pick a time later today—or even tomorrow—to get together. She needed to switch her airline tickets again. Or maybe she should just cancel them altogether and rebook once she knew how long she'd be here.

Her university was on Christmas break, so she wasn't due back until the seventh of January.

He crossed the room to where she stood. "What are you doing?"

"Calling a cab. What else? I need to get back to the hotel before I fall on my face."

The corners of his mouth twitched. "Last time it was pitch facedown into your soup."

"Same thing." She tapped the phone display. She wanted to stay right where she was, but she wouldn't make a fool of herself. Or cause him to be uncomfortable. He'd turned her down twice. Nothing had changed, so throwing herself at him would be in horrible taste. He deserved accolades for rescuing her, not a hussy trying to muscle her way into his bed. She wanted him, but it ran deeper than that. Something about being with him completed her in a way she didn't understand, but she didn't question it, either. Explaining the turmoil making her heart beat faster felt quite beyond her, so she hunched over her phone.

Arlen placed a hand across the screen.

"What are you doing?" She pushed at his hand, confused.

A volley of Gaelic buffeted her, Old Gaelic she had to think about. By the time she'd come up with a loose translation, she bent her head over her purse to hide her elation. He wanted her to stay.

Here.

With him.

He'd just asked her not to leave.

Whoa, sweetie. Listen to the man. He said it's easier to protect me if I'm here. I shouldn't read too much into this. Or anything at all.

Determined not to make an ass out of herself, she let him take her hand and lead her up a winding staircase to the second floor and then up a straight one to the third. The house rose around her, almost feeling alive with its priceless collections of statues, crystal, wall-hangings, and thick, woven rugs that absorbed the sound of footsteps.

Everywhere she looked, Arlen's exquisite taste shone through. Not only was each item delicate and beautiful, they'd been placed to maximize their brilliance in juxtaposition to everything else.

He tightened his fingers around hers; his mood was changing from happiness and relief she was staying to anger. Crap. Had she done something wrong? Or was he simply having second thoughts.

Once they crested the landing, she stole a sidelong glance his way. "You're angry. If you've rethought me staying here—"

He swung her to face him, twin fires burning in the

depths of his dark eyes. "Not angry with you. How could I be?"

Oh, honey. Let me count the ways...

She offered half a smile. "Because I'm pigheaded and don't follow instructions very well."

He shocked the hell out of her by saying, "I find those traits refreshing, appealing—"

Something cracked wide open inside her at the unexpected compliments. Maybe it was the witch blood, but she'd never shied away from going after what she wanted. Her resolve to behave frittered away like dust in a staunch wind. Launching herself at him, she threw her arms around his neck and kissed him. His lips were firm and sweet. He tasted of magic and blood and whiskey; the unusual combination stoked her desire. She could have kissed him forever, but she had to make sure it was what he wanted too.

She pinned him with her gaze. "You've turned me down twice, Arlen MacGregor. Send me away a third time, and I'll never trouble you again." She waited, barely daring to breathe. Would he walk away from her this time too?

Emotion rippled across his defined cheekbones and square chin dotted with dark stubble. Disbelief. Joy. Desire. Others she didn't have names for. She'd expected words, but he wrapped her tight against him and crushed his mouth over hers.

She opened her mouth to him and sparred with his tongue, caught up in the simple relief and joy of being desired in return. He wanted her. This time, he wasn't going to turn from her. She felt hunger, craving in how he held her, kissed her, and in the rigid column of flesh pressing into her belly.

They'd just come from a battlefield. Sex and death were linked. People fucked to remind themselves they were still alive, but what was unfolding between them ran far deeper than that. She didn't question how she knew, in the same way she never questioned any of her intuitions.

They'd never failed her.

And they wouldn't start now. Arlen was hers. They were meant to build a life together. She was as sure of it as she'd ever been of anything. He splayed his hands across her back, leaving trails of heat wherever he touched her. She held onto handfuls of his woolen jacket, wishing for the skin that lay beneath.

Breath quickening, her heart knocked against her ribcage. Her nipples hardened where they were crushed against him, and need slicked her labia and upper thighs. He thrust his tongue inside her mouth; she sucked on it like a drowning woman offered air. Magic filled with his Druid, earth-linked scents thickened around them. Heather, gorse, and rain-wet moorlands mingled with the vanilla herb scent she'd always claimed as her own.

The odors were heady, intoxicating. A woman could live on them forever.

His hands slipped lower down her back until he cupped the curves of her ass, snugging her against her hard-on. She wanted to look at him, kiss every centimeter of him from mouth to chest to stomach. If she could wait that long to take his cock into her mouth.

He made a decidedly male sound, somewhere between a growl and a gasp before ripping his mouth from hers. "I will not take you standing in my upper hall, lass. We're both filthy. I'll get the shower going. Unless you'd prefer a tub."

"What I prefer is you. The faster it happens, the better."

He winked broadly and glided into Gaelic. "Nay, ye only think ye want it fast. I know what ye need, and 'tis long, slow loving where ye scream my name and carve it into the headboard because ye canna help yourself."

Kat laughed. It felt good to let mirth roll through her and mingle with desire. "What about you screaming my name, huh? It's not the 1700s anymore. The definition of manly has undergone some serious revisions."

His face split into a grin, and then he laughed along with her. When he got control of himself, he said, "Aye, and thank all the bloody saints for that, eh? 'Twasn't much fun being a man in those days."

"Funner than being a woman," she countered. "No rights. Seen and not heard. Layers of stiff, uncomfortable clothing that only got washed every couple of months. Shall I go on?"

"Nay." He teased a track up her back until he rubbed her neck beneath her tangled hair. "Third door on the left and all the way through to the bathroom."

She hated to let go of him for even long enough to clean up. Maybe because she hesitated, he swept one arm beneath her knees and carried her down the hall and through the indicated door. It opened before them, no doubt prodded by a magical assist.

A large room set into a corner of the upper floor spread before her. Windows spanning two sides offered a warm welcome, or they would if the sun ever came out in northern Scotland. Decorated in earth tones with wall hangings depicting warriors fighting while magic flashed around them, the room felt alive, much as the house did. A bed piled with colorful duvets and pillows was tucked into a corner. The other side of the room held an enormous carved teak desk laden with computer equipment. Behind it sat shelves holding books and scrolls, many of which she assumed were very old.

"It took me a while," she murmured, thinking about her own juncture where modern ran up against ancient.

"What did?" He hadn't shown any sign of letting go of her as he crossed the room.

"To come to terms with medieval scrolls and the fastest computer I can afford coexisting in the same space. It still feels sacrilegious, somehow."

"Know what you mean. We're kindred spirits in that regard. Probably in a whole lot of other ones too." He grinned engagingly and ducked through a door at the end of the room into an expansive bathroom. Acres of hand-painted, cream-colored tiles stretched across ledges and a sunken tub set into the center of the floor. He deposited her on her feet in front of a glassed-in shower enclosure. After sliding her jacket from her shoulders, he draped it over a hook.

She did the same with his coat, stretching onto her toes to drag it off his shoulders. She was too anxious to get to the buttons of his shirt to scoop the tweed coat off the floor, so she left it where it lay. His attention was on her silk blouse. He undid a couple of buttons before dragging his hand downward. The other half dozen buttons gave way, bouncing across the floor.

"I'll buy you another," he said, his voice rough with need.

"Doesn't matter."

She wanted him to sound that way, as if getting down to skin eclipsed everything. She was only partway done with his shirt when he batted her hands away and dragged it over his head, not bothering to undo the rest of it.

Kat's eyes widened at the vista of copper-gold skin. Puckered nipples were surrounded by dark hair. She bent forward and licked one. He made the growling, gasping sound again, so she did the same thing to the other one. His shoulders were studies in lean, shapely muscle that wound down his arms. The tented-out trousers that rode low on his hips accentuated his flat stomach. She shrugged her shirt off her shoulders. Before she could reach around to undo her bra, he beat her to it. As soon as her breasts were free, he undid her pants, patting the zipper before he jerked it down.

She was having a hard time finding words, but that zipper had saved her from being raped, and she understood exactly why he'd patted it. Her pants pooled around her feet, and she remembered her boots.

The heat of his gaze bored into her, kindling need so intense her head spun. "Boots," she mumbled. Arlen knelt before her, undoing each one and steadying her so he could pull them off.

"You're spoiling me," she managed through vocal cords clotted with lust.

"Ye deserve to be spoiled, lass." The husky rasp that had punctuated his last words deepened. He unlaced his boots, toeing them off once he stood.

Kat reached for his belt. Once it was unhooked, she addressed the fastenings on his pants. They slid down his legs, revealing shorts that did nothing to conceal his erection. He was huge, beautiful, perfect. She'd known but laying eyes on him made it real. She reached for him, but he shook his head.

"Into the shower, wench." He pushed his underwear down his legs before making a grab for the thong she'd forgotten about, maybe because it had melded to her. A tug and it joined the rest of their clothing scattered across the tile floor.

The shower was lined with the same beautiful, delicate painted tiles. Kat bet they were worth a fortune. She touched the electronic keypad, and water shot from nozzles above and beside her. Arlen slid in next to her, making adjustments so the spray pattern mostly fell from above.

She wove her arms around him as water beat down on them, but he grasped her wrists, unraveling her hold on him. "We've gotten this far. By god, we're going to wash off all the 1700s muck." He reached over her and pumped liquid soap that smelled heavenly. Roses and mint and cinnamon. Even better, once he'd rubbed his hands together, he slathered the creamy product across her breasts and belly and back, working it into her skin.

"In the interest of expediency," she murmured, almost too hot to think, and took her own handfuls of soap. Touching him was exquisite. His skin came alive beneath her fingertips, and she couldn't resist coating the length of his cock with bubbly suds. After giving her a look that could have melted stone, he turned around, and she worked soap down the length of his back, kneading the muscled globes of his high, tight ass. She'd always loved men's behinds, and his was the finest she'd seen.

He changed the spray's direction, so it blasted them from the sides, washing the sudsy residue away. "Finally"—he cupped one of her breasts, rolling the nipple—"no more waiting."

Bending, he took her breast in his mouth, sucking hard. Sensation shot through her as he moved from breast to breast. She closed a hand around his erection, working him from base to tip and teasing the velvety head. He groaned and straightened, backing her into a corner. Warm ceramic tiles pressed against her back as he lifted her, balancing her thighs on his forearms.

Kat wrapped her thighs around his waist and her arms around his neck. She felt the blunt, huge head of him, pressed against her vault and writhed to draw him inside. True to his earlier words, he plumbed her slowly, ever so slowly, letting her stretch to accommodate his girth. Her clit was so swollen, so distended with lust, she jammed it against him as he sank into her. Before he even hit bottom, she dissolved around him in a flood of heat and contractions.

He crooned to her in Gaelic. Lusty words that had no counterpart in English. She lapped them up, rubbing her hard nipples against his chest. His arm muscles flexed beneath her thighs as he raised her until just the tip of him remained inside. She wanted to scream at him to move, goddammit, but he took his time lowering her back onto him as the shower poured down around them.

She gripped him tighter with her thighs and began a dance of her own. She couldn't manage full thrusts, but she could do half ones. The bottom of each stroke tormented her clit until another climax circled, pushing her toward its crest. Sex, heat, and lust pummeled her from all sides. She'd never been so aroused. Never needed a man this much.

Arlen was moving faster now, his breath hot on her neck as he bit and licked her, moving from her lips to her cheeks to her neck and back again. She grappled with his shoulder blades, raking him with her nails as another climax rocketed through her. She didn't realize she was screaming until her voice echoed back to her.

Deep inside her, his cock swelled, reaching places she'd never been touched before. He was still crooning in Gaelic, but his tone turned urgent. He was telling her to come once more.

Now.

With him.

Maybe he'd leveraged magic, but his engorged cock pushed her over the crest once more as it juddered, painting her vault with white-hot semen. They clung to one another for a long time, gasping and panting as their bodies quieted.

Somewhere along the road, the water shut itself off. Or maybe Arlen did it. Her eyes were closed as she held onto him. He lifted her off his still-erect cock and shepherded her out of the shower, wrapping her in a thick, fragrant white towel. He draped another around himself and proceeded to dry her.

Happy. Sated. She didn't protest as he fussed over her, combing out her wet hair. She might have dozed during the hair part because she didn't remember him picking her up again or laying her down in his bed.

Her eyes felt heavy, but she forced them open. Thickly feathered duvets with high-thread-count covers plumped around her.

He kissed her forehead. "Sleep, *mo croix*, I'll keep ye save from harm."

"But what about you?" Concern smote her. He'd

fought Hunters. Killed for her. She should be the one watching over him.

Something shifted in the room, perhaps a trick of the light, but when she looked at Arlen, he'd changed. Not so much as to not be recognizable, but he held an otherworldly aspect. Sharper planes in his face, longer hair, more golden skin. His dark eyes had silvery flecks floating in them.

She frowned, not sure what to ask.

He lay next to her and wrapped her in his arms. "All is well, lass. I am both men. The first wears a glamor to move about more easily in a time where magic has fallen out of favor. Yet, 'tis still me."

"Magic. You'll still teach me magic."

His smile warmed her to her toes. "Wouldna miss it for the world, lassie mine."

Lassie mine.

She liked the sound of that, but her mind and body were done cooperating. She might have told him she loved him before sleep staked a claim to her.

Three Weeks Later

Arlen sat in his home library putting the finishing touches on his part of a joint research paper he and Kat had hatched up. A compare and contrast of four of the major clans, it would shed new light into heretofore murky aspects of how the clans bartered for power advantages. While it alluded to magical elements, he'd left that part purposely open to multiple interpretations.

He was so happy it scared him. Much like every dour Scot who'd walked before him, he didn't trust happiness. Far simpler to content oneself with a lesser goal than to be disappointed.

He'd been wedded to duty, to being the strongest Druid he could and ensuring no harm came to his people. All those things were still in play, but loving

Katerina imbued everything with a delight that saturated every cell in his body. They'd been together constantly since that first day, making love, having deep, intense conversations, making love some more, and snatching the occasional break for food and drink.

Christmas was long past, and they were ensconced in a brand-new year.

Come spring, they'd be married. Katerina was taking a sabbatical year from her university duties and at the end of that time, either she'd accept a faculty position at Stirling, or apply to one of the other schools in the U.K.

They'd discussed relocating to the continent—or moving to the Bay Area—but he needed to remain close to his Druid group. Sean, Morgan, and the others had stopped by to check up on them, but they'd exercised admirable restraint and not made pests of themselves. At one point, Sean had drawn him aside and asked pointblank if he was moving to the States. He hadn't bothered to mask his relief when Arlen told him no.

Arlen understood perfectly. Sean had no desire to take over leadership for the group. He would if he had to, but it wasn't his first choice. He was happiest with his head buried in columns of numbers in a quiet corner of his bank.

The research project spread across Arlen's display

was the first of half a dozen. Both he and Katerina hoped by the time they were done, they'd be viewed as such a robust academic asset, they could write their own ticket. They already had reputations as innovative researchers, so combining their knowledge and skillsets made sense.

The sound of Kat's voice raised in exasperation reached him from downstairs. Who the hell was she arguing with? He hurried out of the library and pelted down two flights of stairs to investigate.

"For the second time, why not?" Kat spun circles in the air with the hand not holding her cellphone. After a brief pause, she continued. "Look, Mother. I understand why I didn't get a full report on great-great grannie when I was nine, but I'm long since grown up. Why are you still refusing to even admit she's a witch?"

Arlen covered the remaining distance to her. "Does your mum know Rhea dragged you back in time?"

Kat rolled her eyes and nodded. "She doesn't believe me."

He held his hand out for the phone. This woman would be his mother-in-law. No time like the present to introduce himself.

Kat handed the phone over. He clicked the speaker button and said, "Hello. Lovely to make your acquaintance."

A long, breathy sigh was followed by, "I'm wishing

it was equally 'lovely' to make yours. Something about you has brought the wrath of Hell down on my child. You have to send her back to California. Immediately."

"Christ, Mother." Kat wasn't quite shouting, but almost. "This has nothing to do with Arlen. Like I told you, a Roskelly died. And I bet you know exactly which one it was. The others were counting on her to produce more witches. Now there's only me. It's why—"

"Guard your words, child. You sound like a madwoman."

"Not to me, Mrs. Roskelly," Arlen cut in.

"My last name is Curtis," she said briskly.

Arlen quirked a brow Kat's way, and she tossed her hands skyward. "Mom never liked being a Roskelly, so she changed her name."

He smothered a snort before it could escape and bit back Shakespeare's quote about a rose by any other name. "Fine. Mrs. Curtis, it is." Arlen didn't aim to be diverted by inconsequentials.

"Ms. Liliana Curtis."

He considered asking Kat if her mother was always this cantankerous, but it didn't make any difference. No matter what the answer, she was his wife-to-be's kinswoman and deserving of latitude—if not respect.

He changed the subject. "Did Kat tell you we're getting married? We've selected the Vernal Equinox as being most auspicious. The ceremony will be on the Isle of Skye in one of the old circles of standing stones. It would be wonderful if you could be there. I know it would mean the world to your daughter."

A barrage of crackling static hissed through the phone. Kat's mum hadn't said a word, but her magic was probably wreaking havoc with the electronics.

Determined to get through to the woman, Arlen plowed on. "I'm hoping you'll offer us your blessing." He exchanged a look with Kat, at a loss for what to say next. He didn't want to start out on a poor footing with his beloved's mother.

"Am I correct the two of you have me on speaker phone?" Liliana asked after the silence had spanned several uncomfortably long moments.

"Yeah, Mom. That's right."

"Good. I want you to hear this too. You must return home. The sooner the better." Liliana's voice was higher than it had been and sounded strained.

"I heard you the first time you said that," Kat replied. "What I can't figure out is why. What's so important about me being in California?"

"Not just in California." Her mother paused for emphasis. "In California by yourself." She stressed the by yourself part, leaving zero space for misinterpretation.

Still holding onto the phone, Arlen sank to the

edge of a leather sofa and blew out a breath. "How is it ye doona like me? Ye've not had the chance to meet me." His brogue had thickened, which told him how exasperated he was.

"Oh, child." Liliana's tone softened fractionally. "It's not you. Or maybe it is but only in a peripheral sense. Kat needs to be here to be safe. Why is that so difficult to understand?"

"Child, is it?" He'd be damned if he'd sit still while she patronized him. Nice flew out the window right alongside courteous. "Witches live long lives, Ms. Curtis, but I'll stand ye a hundred quid note I'm far older than you."

"I am not a wit—"

Arlen focused a powerful truth spell and switched to Gaelic since he was close to positive she'd understand. "Aye, ye are indeed a witch. Try to deny your blood. If ye do, 'twill grow quite uncomfortable."

Kat squatted in front of him and tugged on his arm. "Don't hurt her."

"I won't," he mouthed.

A muffled snarl blasted through the phone. "Katerina."

"Front and center, Mom."

"I've devoted my life to keeping your great-great grandmother's claws out of you. Didn't you think it odd I never married? Between gran and me, we maintained a safe margin around you. And you've just blown it all to hell. Don't you understand?" Her voice rose to a shriek. "She knows where you are now. She won't rest until—"

"Stop right there." Arlen infused authority into his words, the same power he used to corral unruly Druids. "I love your daughter. She will be my wife. Mother of our children. Do you think I would let aught happen to her?"

"Pfft. What could you possibly do?"

"Didn't get around to telling her about you," Katerina murmured.

"I heard that. Telling me what?" Liliana demanded.

Arlen unclenched his jaw. He wasn't used to revealing what he was. Those who needed to know were well aware of his position—and his power. Yet, there was no reason to drape his rank in secrecy, either. "I am the arch Druid in all the British Isles, a post I've held since the early 1800s. Between me and my followers, our power is sufficient to keep your daughter from harm."

A strangled intake of breath was followed by, "I'm so very sorry. Can ye ever forgive my impertinence," in stilted Gaelic. After a brief pause, she added in English, "Daughter. You should have told me."

"When would I have had the chance?" Kat asked

dryly. "You were so busy reading me the riot act, it didn't leave much space for anything else."

"This goes against a pact I made with my own mother," Liliana spoke slowly, "but when we next see one another, I owe you a rather long conversation."

"Why did the two of you go to such lengths to keep me in the dark?"

"We had good reasons, but they'll have to wait until we're together. I'll not risk such a conversation to modern electronics."

"Good enough. I can wait." Kat nodded abruptly.

"You will come to our nuptials?" Arlen urged. "Your daughter talked me into the entire masculine portion of the wedding party donning kilts."

"Kilts, eh? Tough to turn down an opportunity like that. I'd be delighted to attend—if you still want me there."

"Of course, we do," Arlen said. "I'm looking forward to meeting you. I understand more than you think about magical secrets and living two lives. One in the 'normal' world and the other in a secret spot where you go to great lengths to avoid discovery."

Kat leaned closer to the phone. "Come sooner than March, Mom. Please. I want you to meet Arlen and see his house. It's this wonderful old place that—"

"Our house," he corrected her.

Liliana chuckled. "I'm liking you more with each passing moment. Probably a good time to hang up."

"Aye, while I still have a toe in positive territory?"

"Something like that. I love you, Kat. See you soon. Maybe sooner than you'd like."

"Not possible, Mom. Plan on staying with us. There are enough rooms here to house an army."

"We'll see. I may book a room. Houseguests and fish both begin to smell after three days. Bye for now."

The connection clicked off, and Arlen started to laugh. "Can't say as I've heard that expression before." He exhaled briskly. "For a moment there, I was afraid all was lost."

"Me too. Not lost, exactly, but Mom has a hellacious temper. I expected her to tell me I'd made my own bed and slam down the phone." Kat settled onto the floor in front of him with her back against his legs. "In truth, I'm shocked she capitulated. It was your Druid disclosure. Why on earth would she be so overwhelmed by it?"

He slid off the couch and sat behind her, wrapping his arms around her and cradling her against him. "Druids are the only weapon left against evil. If your mum identifies as a witch—and let's assume she does— it's been one of those behind closed doors, dark of night relationships. Even so, she'd recognize Druid power as a key element keeping her wicked kinfolks in line."

"Probably right. I hate to admit it, but you usually are."

He grinned. "Now there's a piece of progress. Music to my ears, darling."

"Speaking of progress, how's your part of our paper coming along?"

"Mostly finished. I need to look up a few more references."

She snorted. "Only because you can't tell the truth about where your knowledge came from. Having been there confers quite an edge."

"I've tried not to take undue advantage of it. The hardest part about living so long is when I have to drop out of sight and start over as someone else. It's grown far harder what with fingerprints and National Insurance numbers and DNA. I tell ye, lass, I guard my blood closely. No doctors or hospitals for me."

"I've been thinking about that. The living a long time thing." She leaned her head against his chest. "I suppose I'll be around as long as my other witchy kin." She shook her head. "Wonder when Mom was going to get around to telling me that part? Hell, I wonder how old she is?"

"The other woman in that vision of yours I intercepted. Your grandmother. Is she still alive?"

Kat twisted her head to look at him and drew her brows together. "I have no idea. I attended her funeral, but that might not mean much other than she faked her death."

"Something else to ask your mum about."

"The list is long." She grinned. "Were you done working for today?"

"I could be. What'd you have in mind?"

"We might go out to dinner—later. I really liked that East Indian place."

He keyed into her wording. "If dinner is later, what's now?"

She turned in his arms, a wicked smile in place. Whenever she looked like that, she reminded him of a reincarnation of Aphrodite, and his response was immediate.

They'd had so much sex, he had tender places, but he wasn't complaining. Ever accommodating, his cock swelled, well on its way to a full-blown erection. He cupped both her breasts and rubbed her nipples through the wool of her sweater.

"Aye, lassie?"

She wriggled a hand between them and curved her fingers around his swelling appendage. "We could make love, but first I have something to show you."

"So long as it involves removing all your clothes, I'm all for it."

She let go of him and twisted out of his arms. "Patience, darling."

Something between a groan and a growl bubbled from him. "I used to consider myself a patient man—but 'twas before you came along."

Kat rolled to her feet. "Back in a flash."

"I could follow you. That way, we'll be closer to a bed."

Silvery laughter followed her exit from the great room, but she didn't take him up on his offer, so he remained where he sat.

True to her word, she reappeared in the archway at the far end of the room, her long, dark skirt swirling around her stocking-clad feet. "I have a surprise for you."

He cocked his head to one side, cataloguing different ways to have sex. Not that they'd missed many. "What kind of surprise?"

"You'll find out." She stopped by the bar and selected a bottle of red wine and two long-stemmed goblets. Tucking the bottle beneath one arm, she picked up a corkscrew and returned to where he sat leaning against one of the room's many sofas.

Before she joined him on the floor, she turned and stared at the fireplace. The wood smoldered and sputtered before a small flame wound through it. Kat stared harder at the fire until it was burning nicely.

"Nicely done." He took the wine and glasses from her. "You've quite an aptitude for magic."

She shrugged, looking pleased. "I have the very best teacher of all."

He chuckled. "Aren't we the original mutual admiration society."

She settled next to him, and he took the corkscrew from her and proceeded to open the wine. After a quick glance at the label, he whistled. "Thirty-year-old cab. This must be a special occasion." Pouring the fragrant dark liquid into the goblets, he handed her one.

"It is." Kat nodded and clinked her glass against his. "To us."

"A solid toast, lass." He drank deeply, savoring the complex flavors in the fine, old Cabernet.

Kat set her glass aside and reached into a pocket, withdrawing an oblong box wrapped in tissue. Color splotched her cheeks, and she smiled softly. "I bought you a gift. To celebrate our engagement."

He waited, but she still clutched the box. "Are ye planning on giving it to me?" He switched to Gaelic. "Or will ye just tease me with it?"

The color across her cheekbones deepened. "I guess I'm afraid you won't like it." She thrust the box into his lap.

Arlen placed his glass next to hers on a nearby table. Curious about her gift and touched she'd gone to the effort of selecting something, he pulled the tissue aside, revealing an ancient-looking wooden box carved with sacred Druidic runes. His heart beat faster as he unlatched a brass fastener. Nestled within were two golden rings—one larger, one smaller—set with faceted red stones that reflected light off their surfaces. Next to the rings was a necklace of finely woven gold. Craftsmanship like that had died out of the world long ago.

Kat was watching him, her heart in her eyes. "I bought our wedding rings. Do you like them? They're not too much? Sean said you have a pendant that goes with the necklace." She looked down. "I'm babbling. Sorry."

Emotion spilled through Arlen, thickening his throat. "Lass. These cost a fortune. Ye shouldna have—"

She held up a hand. "Do you like them? More importantly, are you angry I didn't consult you about our rings?"

"How could I be angry? They're beautiful. I love them, but not nearly as much as I love you." He held out his arms.

She scooted into them and plucked the larger ring out of its silk-lined cradle. "Hold out your hand," she said and slipped it into place on his finger. "Excellent. It fits."

"How could it not?" he retorted. "If Sean

mentioned the pendant, he must have told you these rings were cast with magic."

"He did, but I wasn't certain I believed him." She paused a beat. "So you recognize them?"

"Indeed, I do. These rings graced the hands of the first Druid lord and his lady. How Sean found them is anyone's guess."

Kat gifted him with a Mona Lisa smile. "Maybe he had them all along."

Arlen laughed. "Knowing Sean, perhaps he did. The man is nothing if not a packrat."

Her smile broadened.

"You are so lovely, he murmured, "Have I told you lately how beautiful you are?"

"Not in the last hour or two."

He tightened his arms around her and brought his mouth down atop hers. Her body came alive against his, and passion pounded through him. The air developed an iridescent hue as magic spiraled outward from where they sat, kissing one another.

He raised his mouth from hers long enough to say, "Ye're mine, lassie."

"Nay," she corrected him, aping his brogue. "We belong to each other."

You're reached the end of *Timespell,* first of the Elemental Witch books. I do hope you've enjoyed it. Please leave a review while the book is fresh in your mind. Doesn't have to be fancy. A line or two will do it.

Time's Curse, next of the Elemental Witch books will join this one soon. There's a lot to explore in this world of witches and Druids. Meanwhile, if you're hooked on Scotland and time travel, you'll love my Dragon Lore books. A sample from *Highland Secrets,* the first volume from that series follows.

ABOUT THE AUTHOR

Ann Gimpel is a USA Today bestselling author. A lifelong aficionado of the unusual, she began writing speculative fiction a few years ago. Since then her short fiction has appeared in many webzines and anthologies. Her longer books run the gamut from urban fantasy to paranormal romance. Once upon a time, she nurtured clients. Now she nurtures dark, gritty fantasy stories that push hard against reality. When she's not writing, she's in the backcountry getting down and dirty with her camera. She's published over sixty books to date, with several more planned for 2018 and beyond. A husband, grown children, grandchildren, and wolf hybrids round out her family.

Keep up with her at www.anngimpel.com or http://anngimpel.blogspot.com

If you enjoyed what you read, get in line for special offers and pre-release special reads. Newsletter Signup!

Furious and weary, Angus Shea wants out, but no matter how he feels, he can't stop the magic powering his visions. The Celts kidnapped him when he wasn't much more than a boy and forced him to do their bidding. He's sick of them and their endless assignments, but they wiped his memories, and he has no idea where he came from.

Dragon shifters are disappearing from the Scottish Highlands, and the Celtic Council sends Angus to investigate. He meets up with Arianrhod, legendary virgin huntress from Celtic myth, in Fire Mountain, the dragons' home world.

Arianrhod prefers to work alone, mostly because she harbors a dirty little secret and guards her privacy for the best of reasons. She's not exactly a virgin, and she'd be laughed out of the Pantheon if the truth surfaced. Despite the complications of leading a double life, she's never found a lover who tempted her to walk away from her fellow Celtic gods.

Attraction ignites, hot and so urgent Arianrhod's carefully balanced life teeters on the brink of discovery. Angus is everything she's ever wanted, but he's far too close to her Celtic kin to keep her secret safe. Angus wants her too, but she's a Celt. He's hated them forever, and she's part of everything he's lain awake nights plotting to escape from.

Can they risk everything?

Will they?

If they do, can they live with the consequences?

Angus Shea stroked beneath icy waters off the northern tip of Ireland, blending his energy with a pod of Selkies. The sea creatures cut through choppy waves in front, behind, and above him. He'd rather dive and play in the deeps with them—and if it were any other day, he would have—but he needed to keep an eye on the skies, so he edged toward the surface, pushing his head free.

Celene, a coal black Selkie he'd done more than swim with, drew close enough her lush pelt stroked his skin. He draped an arm around her, and she nuzzled his neck with her snout.

"Where have you been?" She spoke deep into his mind. Accommodating vocal chords were part of her human form, not her seal, and he'd never learned the Selkies' lyrical language.

"I spent a little time at my home in Scotland, but mostly I've ranged far from the Irish Sea."

"That doesn't tell me anything." She nipped playfully at his shoulder with her squared-off teeth.

"Prying ears are everywhere." He leaned into her warmth, enjoying a respite from the cold water.

"We could go where no one would hear."

He was tempted, so tempted he toyed with saying yes and taking a break from watching for the dragon he expected. Dragons interpreted time in their own way, and the damned thing might not show up today or tomorrow or even this week. If it showed at all.

How much could he tell the Selkie?

An answer crowded on the heels of his question.

Nothing.

Angus shuttered his mind, so the creature swimming by his side couldn't read it. Much as he yearned to talk with someone, anyone, about the impossibilities the gods tasked him with, prudence won out. Not that this assignment was worse than any of the others, but he'd finally figured out they'd never end.

I could say no. Tell them I'm done.

He cut off the bitter laugh that wanted out. Whoever had the balls to refuse the Celts risked swift and certain punishment. He could hear Gwydion, master enchanter, or Ceridwen, goddess of the world, laughing their heads off—before they cut out his tongue or killed him on the spot.

"You don't have to say a word." Celene went on, almost as if she'd peeked into his thoughts before he took care to protect them. Selkie laughter buffeted him, spraying him with a warm, rich melody mixed with salty water. *"I'm curious, but I miss your body."*

He missed hers too. She'd been his only break from solitude for more years than he wanted to admit. He cast another glance skyward. Though he tried to be subtle, he heard a smug murmur near his ear and knew he hadn't fooled the Selkie.

"You wait for an Ancient One." The tenor of her mind speech shifted as she shielded it from anyone who might be close. Without stopping for him to corroborate, she forged ahead. *"We can take up the banner and watch for you. My kin will let us know."*

Angus picked his way carefully, as if he walked through a field of unexploded ordnance. "I appreciate the thought, but no one can know of my comings or goings, lass."

"We know more than you think." Celene batted him with a flipper. *"In truth, very little escapes us, but here isn't the place to share what I heard about your latest mission."*

Concern rippled through him. If the Selkies knew, who else might? Hell, he didn't know much beyond his assigned meeting place with the dragon, and they'd be heading into danger.

What else was new? Danger was so second nature, his adrenaline pumps barely flinched at anything these days.

"Come with me." Either Celene was oblivious to the turmoil rumbling through him, or she ignored it. She swam from beneath his arm and herded him toward shore. *"There's a secluded glade deep in marsh grass. No one will find us, and my kin will keep watch for the dragon. I already asked."*

The Selkies would do their best—and maybe today it would be enough—but they were no match for evil that had sunk its roots deep into the fabric of the Old Country and the rest of this world. It was why the gods stooped to using him—half-mortal, half-divine, or whatever the hell he was—to do their dirty work. Arawn, god of the dead, revenge, and terror, caught him skulking in the time-travel tunnels when he wasn't much more than a boy and trapped him, cutting off any possibility of return. To make certain Angus remained, the god altered his memories, so he had no idea where he came from.

Now almost twenty-five years later, Arawn and the others still came up with enough for him to do that a life to call his own was out of the question. The carrot they dangled was the truth about his birth, but they never came close to divulging it. The stick was his fear of what they'd do, if he told them he was done.

Over time, he'd stopped asking about his origins. He cared, but it wasn't worth the energy to run up against their stony faces and cunningly crafted half-truths that revealed exactly nothing. Despite his reservations about a quick dalliance with Celene—and maybe missing his rendezvous with the dragon—he was sick of his self-imposed isolation.

She chivied him into shallow water. Once she was certain he'd follow, she drew ahead easily. As if the other Selkies understood, the pod dispersed. When he peered through gray-green water for their multi-colored pelts, they weren't there.

By the time he clambered onto the rocky shore, Celene had shucked her skin. In human form, she opened her arms to welcome him. Long black hair shrouded her almost to her feet. Violet eyes gleamed in welcome. Her generous breasts peeked through the curtain of hair, their copper-colored nipples already pebbled with wanting him.

Angus had tucked his clothes beneath a rock before joining the Selkie pod. Because he swam nude, nothing was in the way as he plunged into Celene's offered embrace. God, how he'd missed the touch of another against him, skin to skin. Celene's body felt warm against his chilled one. She closed her arms around him and ran her hands down his back, lingering over the curve of his butt.

He hugged her in return. The scent of her, salt and mint, flooded his mind with images of their lovemaking, and his cock hardened between their bodies. He trailed his fingertips down her smooth skin, marveling at how different she felt from a human woman. Velvety and charged with electricity. Some Selkies walked among humans, even took permanent partners. Angus didn't understand how they eluded discovery.

Celene closed her mouth over the junction between his neck and shoulder, licking, sucking, biting. He moved a hand from her back to cup the side of her face and lowered his lips over hers. Desire engulfed him. Hot, urgent, desperate, he sank his tongue into her waiting mouth.

She grappled with his ass, pulling his body hard against hers as her hips writhed and breath hitched in her throat. Tearing her mouth from his, she gasped. "Too long. It's been too long."

Liquid heat trailed the path of her mouth as she licked her way down his chest, stopping to tease his nipples. He kissed the top of her head and wove his fingers into her long hair. Every nerve came alive with wanting her, but it ran deeper than that. Touch was such a basic need, and he'd denied that essential part of his humanity—along with every other comfort.

For what?

No matter how much he gave the Celts, they took every shred—and him—for granted. He wanted to get a job, blend in with humans. Something mundane like driving a cab, or flipping burgers in a grill, but his requests were denied. The Celts provided for him. So long as they housed and fed him, why would he need to clutter his time with anything as humdrum as earning a living? What if they needed him, and he was in the middle of washing dishes in some nameless restaurant? He could almost hear Gwydion's voice. See the master enchanter with a long-suffering look on his face—

He wiped his Celtic masters from his mind. This time was for him and Celene. No one else belonged in his head. Just because he'd chosen a semimonastic existence was no reason he couldn't give her everything she needed. Months had passed since they'd last been together, maybe as much as a year. He moved back enough to fill his hands with her breasts, rubbing her erect nipples before he bent to suck on them, remembering the little biting motions she loved.

A low, guttural moan escaped her, and she threaded her fingers through his hair. Holding him against her breasts, she began to sing as he loved her. A series of low, sweet notes rose in cadence and intensity as she lost herself in his touch. He'd asked her about the music once, and she told him it was how sea people vocalized their joy. The music filled him with unbearable hunger—poignant, mind-bending need for another person's touch.

Although he'd never done it before, he raised his voice and joined her song. The change was instantaneous. In that moment, he sensed her loneliness and isolation, twin to his own and recognized that both of them needed more kisses, more touches—even more than they needed sex.

"Lay on your belly." His voice rasped with wanting her. He tore tufts of marsh grass and arranged them to make her a bed on a sandy stretch between rocks.

She lay down, continuing to sing. Angus sang too, as he straddled her and ran his hands down her back rubbing tension from her muscles. He followed his hands with his mouth and strung kisses across her shoulder blades and down the line of vertebrae from her neck to the curves of her ass. Between their song, the feel of her skin beneath his fingertips, and his cock getting stiffer by the moment, waiting became almost painful, yet he held back, not quite sure why.

The rhythm and cadence of her song shifted as he alternated his mouth and hands across the sculpted planes of her back. The intense pressure in his balls receded almost as if he'd reached a peak, though he hadn't come. Maybe she sensed his need for warmth, contact, much as he'd sensed hers.

"Move off me so I can look at you." Celene flipped over to face him, kneeling above her. Rose and gold splotched her pale skin, and a broad smile split her exotic, high-cheek-boned face. "Today was different. You sang with me. You've never done that before."

He shrugged, suddenly self-conscious. "It felt right. Even though I wasn't inside you, what happened between us felt right."

She cocked her head to one side and trained her gaze on him. "Are you sure you don't have sea blood?"

A flicker of annoyance at the Celts' staunch refusal to disclose anything about his birth narrowed his eyes. "I have no idea what I am." He ticked what he did know off on his fingers. "I'm not immortal, but I'll live well beyond human lifespans. My magic is closer to seer and witch than anything else, yet I'm neither of those. The covens acknowledge me as one of theirs, but only because the local witches are too kind to tell me to go away. The time-travel portals accept me." He shrugged again. "I don't suppose knowing more would make a hell of a lot of difference."

"You're not from Scotland, even though you live there." She stated it baldly, as fact.

He frowned. "Why would you say that?"

"Your speech. There's something about the lilt of Scotland that's impossible to rid yourself of. You don't sound Irish or British, either, at least not from the time we live in." Her nostrils flared. "Maybe that's it."

"Maybe what's it?"

"You could be from the past, and not just a few years back, perhaps hundreds—or even more. I'm not old enough to recall what human speech sounded like then, but some Selkies are."

"Fine." Frustration tightened his chest, like it always did when the mystery of his origins became a point of discussion. "My first memories are when the god of the dead dragged me out of a time-travel portal when I was fifteen."

"I'm sorry." She draped a hand over his hip, cradling it. "I've upset you."

He started to protest, but she silenced him with a look. "Don't insult me with a lie, Angus, but you don't have to talk about it, either. Such a pretty man." She stroked hair back from his face. "With your deep brown hair and amber eyes. Did you know they shade to dark gold when you're angry?"

She was trying to divert him with flattery, but he wasn't buying it. "You have no idea what it's like not knowing—" He shook his head, and the rest of his words died unspoken. It didn't matter what she knew or didn't know about him. She'd never be more than an occasional lover, and both of them knew it.

"It could be more," she said softly, obviously having been in his mind.

Angus took her hands in his and gazed at her. "You get more of me than anyone, and you see how pathetically little that is. There's nothing more to give."

"There could be," she persisted. "You could refuse next time they send you on—"

He bent toward her and laid a hand over her mouth. "I'm not free. Not now. Not ever."

"I don't understand." She pushed his hand away and closed very white teeth over her full lower lip.

He smiled crookedly. "Not sure I do, either. Every man has a life's work. No matter how I feel about it, this appears to be mine."

Even though it wasn't wise, he started to ask what she knew about his current assignment, but a flash of unusual energy drew his gaze skyward. He leapt to his feet. A copper-colored dragon circled to land not far from him. Maybe the Ancient One had seen him with Celene and decided to be considerate.

Not very fucking likely. Dragons were a force unto themselves.

"I have to go," he said. "Let me walk you to your skin, so I know you're safely on your way home."

A sad expression crossed her face, creasing the skin

around her eyes into a network of fine lines. "It's right here." She scrambled to her feet and gripped both his upper arms, forcing him to look at her. "Thank you."

"For what?"

"Being you." She brushed her lips over his and moved to a marsh grass thicket. In moments, she'd dragged her pelt over her human body. Transformed into a seal, she waded into the surf.

Before it engulfed her, she turned to gaze at him. *"Be careful, and think on what I said."*

He didn't answer, just watched her head bob in the waves before turning toward his clothing. It wasn't far from the place Celene had led them. His body felt vibrant, alive, and he still tingled from her touch. He longed for a woman of his own, children, a home, before he stuffed the impossible so deep under wraps he couldn't mourn the loss.

Angus moved the large rock he'd placed over his clothes to protect them from the wind. He pulled a ragged dark blue fisherman's knit sweater over his head and stepped into thick, black woolen trousers. Settling on a log, he pulled on socks and laced up stout leather boots. Though the breeze was raw, he'd worn neither hat nor gloves.

Ready as he figured he'd ever be, he covered the fifty yards to where the dragon had settled up the beach. He didn't recognize this one, but he'd only met a bare handful of the hundreds living in Fire Mountain and on other worlds as well. When he drew near, he stopped and bowed his head respectfully, waiting for the dragon to speak first.

"I don't like this any better than you do," the dragon muttered. "Come close enough I don't have to broadcast our business to the world."

Angus walked closer. He could've suggested the dragon use telepathy since all the Ancient Ones were conversant in the technique, but he kept his mouth shut. The dragon was smaller than many he'd seen. Copper scales shaded to burnished gold on its chest, and dark eyes with golden centers whirled so fast they held a hypnotic quality. Lethal, six-inch-long red claws tipped its stubby forelegs. The dragon stood upright on hind legs tipped with the same sharp claws and kept its gaze averted, not saying anything.

What the hell? Every other dragon he'd met was proud, imperious, and quick to remind Angus of his inferiority. This one seemed young, but was it? After another long few minutes, Angus tossed respect—and caution—to the winds.

"What's your name? And what are we supposed to be doing? All Ceridwen told me was to meet you here."

The dragon opened its mouth, and a gout of flame landed scant inches from Angus's boots.

He frowned and drew his brows together. "If we're

going to work together, I need to know what to call you." He sent a speculative gaze across the air between them. "If you annihilate me, they'll just assign you a new partner, and I'm a hell of a lot easier to get along with than any of the Celts."

"Tell me something I don't know," the dragon rumbled and belched smoke.

Frustration in its voice struck a note in Angus's soul, and he gestured with both hands. "You may as well tell me who you are and what we're supposed to do together." He infused his words with subtle persuasion. If the dragon didn't care for the Celts, either, they'd likely get along well enough.

"Why? What I should do is leave." The dragon sounded sulky—and scared.

"If you could, you'd already be gone." Angus was as certain of that as he was of anything. The dragon needed him for something, and whatever it was, the Ancient One wasn't particularly proud of it. "What happened? Am I some sort of punishment for you?" Tension settled like a steel bar across his shoulders, and he curled his hands into fists before he realized what he'd done.

"Oh I'd be gone, would I?"

The dragon ignored Angus's questions, and it mimicked his tone with eerie precision. It furled its wings and flapped them a time or two. Dirt swirled;

small pebbles slapped Angus in the face. The creature belched steam and looked so distraught, he felt sorry for it.

"My life's not exactly a picnic, either," he ventured, on a hunt for common ground. "I'm a permanent mercenary, with no time off and no possibility of parole."

That got the dragon's attention, and it focused its whirling gaze on him. The golden centers of its eyes deepened with fiery motes that looked like little shooting stars. "Why would you want a respite from being a warrior?"

Good question.

"Because I'm tired. I'd like what most men have."

"What's that?" The dragon raised its brows, and its scales clanked against each other in a dissonant tinkling.

He shook his head. "It doesn't matter. The sooner you spit out whatever you need to say, the easier it'll be. The worst part about holding something you're ashamed of inside is it eats at you until you're nothing but a hollow shell."

Wings flapped, and those intense, whirling eyes shifted to the rocky beach. "I'm not *ashamed* of anything. I've been banished. Ceridwen said if I worked with you—and we were successful—I might be able to return."

Angus kept surprise out of his voice. "Banished from Fire Mountain?"

Steam puffed from the dragon's open mouth. "No. Idiot. I could live with that. They've banished me from the Highlands. My home."

"What happened?"

"It doesn't matter." The dragon threw his words back at him. "We have to go to Fire Mountain, where I'm to find one of the First Born. Once we have him —or her—"

"One of the six First Born dragons?" Angus broke in, scarcely believing the dragon's words. "They'll never show themselves—unless it's in their best interest."

Another wing flap and a defiant head toss. "There are actually ten. One of them was my father."

"When's the last time you saw him?" The words slipped out before he could stop them. Dragon males frequently didn't hang about once mating was over with, but the trembling mass of scales in front of him likely didn't need to be reminded.

"Never. Mother said he was too immersed in battles on another world to return for our hatching."

Angus unclenched his fists and hunted for something soothing to say that wasn't an outright lie. Dragon energy poked past his wards and into his mind. He tried to block it, but couldn't.

"You believe locating a First Born is hopeless." The dragon sounded resigned. "I may as well throw myself into a crater at Fire Mountain. I'll never see the Highlands again—or my mate." More wing rustling and the dragon rose a few feet off the ground, clearly intent on leaving.

"Hold on." Angus loped forward until he was right beneath the dragon. "I didn't say that—or think it, either. I don't know enough to make any sort of judgment. How about if you start at the beginning? If we're going to work together, I deserve that much."

The dragon circled a few times, indecision stamped in its erratic flight pattern.

"I know what it is to be alone." He kept his voice gentle. "And to not have anyone who cares if I live or die."

Maybe it wasn't totally true. Celene might shed a tear or two, but she'd be the only one. He kept his gaze trained on the sky, relieved the dragon wasn't putting distance between them. Something about the creature's pain tugged at his heart and made it feel like a kindred spirit.

The copper dragon folded its wings and settled heavily to earth a few feet from where Angus stood. It straightened its shoulders and tipped its chin defiantly.

"My name is Eletea," the dragon announced, revealing its gender.

"Angus Shea, though you likely know that."

"Yes, I do. I killed a mage, who fancied herself a dragon shifter." Eletea's eyes whirled faster, as if she dared Angus to say something.

He crinkled his forehead as he dredged up what he knew about dragon shifters. "Don't mages take their chances when they show up seeking a dragon to pair with?"

She nodded once, sharply. "The mage seduced one of us into believing her. I saved him by killing her, but he turned on me. Reported me to the Dragons' Council, and they roped the Celts into deciding my fate, since the one I killed had Celtic blood." Eletea's scales rippled in the dragon equivalent of a shrug. "I don't understand why they're bothering. It's not like I went after one of the gods. They're immortal. The one all the fuss is over barely qualified as a Celt."

Angus kept his expression neutral. "Celtic blood aside, I thought mages only bonded with same sex dragons."

"That was another problem," Eletea said, sounding vindicated. "No one saw it but me, though."

Sensing the worst was out on the table, Angus settled on a nearby rock and invited, "Start at the beginning. We have time."

"No, we don't," Eletea protested. "We should've been at Fire Mountain yesterday." She hung her head.

"I didn't know what I wanted to do, so I flew and flew and flew. I almost didn't land this afternoon."

Angus did his best to project optimism. "Let's open a time-travel portal and be on our way to Fire Mountain." At the dragon's reluctant nod, he went on. "I understand you have your own ways of returning home, but if you travel with me, you can fill me in as we go."

What he didn't say was it probably wouldn't matter when they arrived at the dragons' home world. First Borns wouldn't give them the time of day, whether they showed up early, late, or right on time. He held many concerns, such as what would a First Born do, assuming they could locate one? But he held those cares inside for now.

He could've dreamed the future. Instead, he summoned a spell to take them to a time-traveling portal. Once the undulating gray-pink tube admitted them, he gradually paid out questions.

Reticent and quiet at first, Eletea finally began to talk.

Series:

Alphas in the Wild

Hello Darkness

Alpine Attraction

A Run for Her Money

Fire Moon

Bitter Harvest

Deceived

Twisted

Abandoned

Betrayed

Redeemed

Coven Enforcers

Blood and Magic

Blood and Sorcery

Blood and Illusion

Demon Assassins

Witch's Bounty

Witch's Bane

Witches Rule

Dragon Lore

Highland Secrets

To Love a Highland Dragon

Dragon Maid

Dragon's Dare

Earth Reclaimed

Earth's Requiem

Earth's Blood

Earth's Hope

Elemental Witch

Timespell

GenTech Rebellion

Winning Glory

Honor Bound

Claiming Charity

Loving Hope

Keeping Faith

Rubicon International

Garen

Lars

Soul Dance

Tarnished Beginnings

Tarnished Legacy
Tarnished Prophecy
Tarnished Journey

Soul Storm

Dark Prophecy

Dark Pursuit

Dark Promise

Underground Heat

Roman's Gold

Wolf Born

Blood Bond

Wolf Clan Shifters

Alice's Alphas

Megan's Mates

Sophie's Shifters

Wylde Magick

Gemstone

Lion's Lair

Unbalanced

Standalone Books:

Branded, That Old Black Magic Romance (paranormal romance)

Edge of Night (short story collection, paranormal and horror)

Grit is a 4-Letter Word (nonfiction)

Heart's Flame (post-apocalyptic romance)

Icy Passage (science fiction romance)
Marked by Fortune (post-apocalyptic coming of
age story)
Melis's Gambit (historical paranormal romance)
Midnight Magic (paranormal romance)
Red Dawn (post-apocalyptic paranormal romance)
Shadow Play (historical paranormal romance)
Shadows in Time (Highland time travel romance)
Since We Fell (contemporary romance)
Warin's War (paranormal romance)